RED DIRT
Diaries

Blue's News

Katrina Nannestad

ABC
Books

The ABC 'Wave' device is a trademark of the
Australian Broadcasting Corporation and is used
under licence by HarperCollins*Publishers* Australia.

First published in Australia in 2012
This edition published in 2014
by HarperCollins*Children'sBooks*
a division of HarperCollins*Publishers* Australia Pty Limited
ABN 36 009 913 517
harpercollins.com.au

HarperCollins*Publishers*
Level 13, 201 Elizabeth Street, Sydney NSW 2000, Australia
Unit D1, 63 Apollo Drive, Rosedale, Auckland 0632, New Zealand
A 53, Sector 57, Noida, UP, India
77–85 Fulham Palace Road, London W6 8JB, United Kingdom
2 Bloor Street East, 20th floor, Toronto, Ontario M4W 1A8, Canada
195 Broadway, New York NY 10007, USA

National Library of Australia Cataloguing-in-Publication entry:

Nannestad, Katrina, author.
  Blue's news / Katrina Nannestad.
  ISBN: 978 0 7333 3396 5 (pbk.)
  Nannestad, Katrina. Red dirt diaries ; 3.
  For primary school age.
  Teachers—Juvenile fiction.
  Journalism—Juvenile fiction.
  Farm life—Juvenile fiction.
  Australian Broadcasting Corporation.
A823.4

Cover design by Hazel Lam, HarperCollins Design Studio
Cover illustrations by Katrina Nannestad; background images by
shutterstock.com
Internal design by Priscilla Nielsen
Typeset by Kirby Jones
Printed and bound in Australia by McPherson's Printing Group
The papers used by HarperCollins in the manufacture of this book are
a natural, recyclable product made from wood grown in sustainable
plantation forests. The fibre source and manufacturing processes meet
recognised international environmental standards, and carry certification.

To Bloss, Sniff and Mouse

RED DIRT
Diaries
Blue's News

Macka

Gunther and
his bunnies

Dad   Mum   Peter   Sophie

Fluffles

Doris

Gertrude

Mildred

Petal

Blue (Me!) Wes Fez Mrs W

April

Monday, 16 April — Start of term two

Today is a very important day in the history of Hardbake Plains. I am so excited!

Mat, Ben and I are starting a newspaper for our big year seven English project. Hardbake Plains has never had a newspaper before. Not even when the population grew to 237 people during the wool boom of the 1800s.

At first Matilda Jane the Mature wasn't going to help. She really wanted us all to create a fashion magazine called *Matilda's Wardrobe*. But then Ben sat on her for one and a half hours and she kindly agreed to do the newspaper instead.

We have already decided that it will be called *The Bake Tribune*. Other papers have grand names like *The Herald*, *The Chronicle* and *The Proclaimer*, so we reckon Hardbake Plains' first ever newspaper should have a special name.

The Bake Tribune
THE BAKE TRIBUNE
The bake tribune

However you write it, it looks terribly important. It's bound to be a success.

Tuesday, 17 April

Our new teacher is arriving on Friday.

The school has had a lot of trouble getting someone to take Miss McKenzie's place while she's in Scotland. Everyone's saying it's because we are so far out west and such a tiny town. But I know it's because people are scared of Wes and Fez. Everyone here is used to them — a bit like people who live in the Swiss Alps are used to avalanches, or people in Kenya are used to lions. But to the outsider, Wes and Fez would seem terrifying, dangerous and strange.

Mr Cluff doesn't make the place look so good either. He's been such a gloomy guts since Miss McKenzie left. He mopes around like a zombie with a toothache. Not a welcoming sight.

I really thought Miss McKenzie would be back by the start of the new term, but she hasn't even mentioned coming home. She might be Scottish by birth, but she really does belong here at Hardbake Plains. She fitted in from the day she arrived. As Dad said, Miss McKenzie became as Aussie as a cockatoo eating a lamington in a gumtree.

We had an executive meeting for *The Bake Tribune* today. Hopefully the first edition will be out in a few weeks. I am going to be the editor and chief reporter. Ben will be the designer and printer. Mat is having trouble deciding on what she wants to contribute, because she is an expert in *so* many areas — fashion, romance, skin care, romance, diets, romance, boarding school, romance ... I suppose she'll sort it out sooner or later.

Petal, my duck, will have to be the editor's paperweight. She has started coming to school with me again. Poor old Mrs Whittington, who lives in our shearers' cottage, gets quite confused at times. She tried to bake Petal for an early Christmas dinner last week, so I don't really feel like she is safe at home without me.

Wednesday, 18 April

Mat has decided that she will write a romance serial for *The Bake Tribune*. She is not quite sure what to call it yet, but it's certain to be something totally embarrassing, like 'Safari into Love' or 'Colliding Hearts'.

She said her trip to the Dubbo Zoo in the school holidays with Warren from Warren has given her plenty of ideas for the love scenes (smirk, blush, giggle …). Apparently she had a million romantic experiences in a single day. Warren grasped her hand every time they were near the tigers (I think that shows he's a big, fat scaredy pants, but Mat assures me it's a sign of deep affection). He gazed into her eyes *five times* near the camels, and kissed her cheek behind the elephants.

Ben was busy doing an online maths challenge and thought Mat said Warren had kissed the cheek of an elephant's behind. Ben has always thought Warren from Warren sounded like a real nerd, but now he's not so sure. Anyone brave enough to kiss an elephant on the butt has Ben's total respect and admiration.

Two days until the new teacher arrives …

Thursday, 19 April

Talked to the whole school about the paper today. They were really excited and liked the idea of being able to contribute their own stuff. Banjo said he'd write some poetry. Tom said he would do a survey like they have on TV in the mornings. Wes and Fez said they would write a regular column on manners (???).

I had a huge argument with Mat this morning. She was drivelling on and on about her romance story so I pointed out that newspapers were meant to print stuff that was *interesting* and *educational*, not just daft stories about women who were so desperately in love that their brains shrank to the size of peanuts.

Mat said that *I* could hardly be a decent journalist and editor because I would make the entire newspaper about farms and sheep and wheat. She said a good editor would have a wide range of interests, *including* romance and girly stuff.

Ben told us to shut up because he was winning an online maths challenge against a girl called Cindy from Menindee, and if he lost he'd sit on both of us until our eyes popped out.

Spent my English lesson researching how to be a great journalist. The main thing is to be adventurous and have *a wide range of interests and experiences*. Matilda Jane the Mature was right! I hate it when that happens!!!

So I took a journalist's oath, right in front of Ben and Mat. I held my favourite pen and notepad in the air and said:

'I, Blue Weston, will be open to trying new things, no matter how scary, dangerous, lame or embarrassing they may seem.'

Ran around the back yard with Wes and Fez all evening, wearing a tea cosy on my head and balancing slugs on my nose. Not *my* idea of fun, but an oath is an oath …

Friday, 20 April

The new teacher has arrived. His real name is Mr Sanders but he likes to be called the Colonel. He's living in Mrs Whittington's old cottage just across the road from the school.

The Colonel is tall and skinny with white legs, knobbly knees and bushy grey eyebrows. He wears shiny black hiking boots and baggy shorts with enormous pockets.

He used to be a Scout leader and wants to do outdoor adventure activities with us — abseiling, archery, fire making and a whole heap of other stuff that Mum would *definitely* not want Wes and Fez to learn about. Even though abseiling sounds exciting, I'm not sure that having the Colonel here is such a good idea. It's awfully lonely without Miss McKenzie, but some knobbly-kneed old Scout leader is hardly going to fill the gap.

Spent lunch time learning to be a worm whisperer. Sam Wotherspoon thinks cheerful worms are the key to a thriving vegie patch, so he is trying to talk his worms to happiness. He said we have horse whisperers and dog whisperers, so why not worm whisperers?

I can think of several pretty good reasons why not, but I *have* taken the journalist's oath, so I lay on my stomach in the dirt, digging up worms, tickling their tummies and telling them how clever they are. Mat and Ben sat on the veranda steps laughing at me, but I felt proud to be having a new experience.

Saturday, 21 April

Wes and Fez spent the morning repainting the sign at the front gate. Everyone knows the Westons live at Hillrose Poo, but Mrs Welsh-Pearson changed the sign to 'Hillrose Park' before Miss McKenzie's wedding-that-never-quite-happened. Mum and Dad said we should leave it that way, but it just didn't seem right. It was too fancy.

Anyway, today Wes and Fez changed it back to Hillrose Poo and painted a brand-new brown blob.

'It's really cool, Blue,' said Wes. 'It's the biggest poo I've ever seen.'

'Except for the poo that elephant did at the circus,' said Fez.

They emailed a picture of it (the sign, not the elephant poo!) to Dougal, Miss McKenzie's little brother, in Scotland. I hope Miss McKenzie sees it and realises how much she misses us all. She has to come back soon, surely … and hopefully before the Colonel gets too settled in.

Sunday, 22 April

Tennis at the Sweeneys' this afternoon. Mum and Mrs O'Donnell beat Mat and me. We should have won by heaps but Mat was too upset to focus on her game. Warren from Warren had sent her an email last night asking why Ben Simpson from Hardbake Plains Public School thinks he kissed an elephant on the bum at the Dubbo Zoo.

'It's so totally embarrassing,' Mat cried. 'Now Warren thinks I told everyone that he likes kissing elephants' bottoms when really he likes kissing me on the cheek.'

I told her not to worry. She just needs to email Warren and explain that it's difficult for Ben to tell the difference between Mat's face and an elephant's bum. It's a common mistake that anyone could have made.

Mat wasn't comforted by this at all. In fact, she seemed a little bit cross.

Oh well, at least I tried.

When we got home, Mrs Whittington was halfway down the driveway, wandering towards the front gate. She was carrying a steamed golden syrup pudding. Our pigs Gertrude, Mildred and Doris were walking slowly by her side. I think they were keeping watch over her.

Mrs Whittington said she was taking the pudding to Blue over at the school, but it seemed a lot further away than she remembered. I suppose that's true. She used to live just across the road from Hardbake Plains Public. Now the school's twenty-five kilometres away. She doesn't remember that she's moved house and now lives in our shearers' cottage, Magpie's Rest.

Mum wanted to drive Mrs Whittington back home, but she wouldn't get in the car without the pigs. So I got out and walked slowly back to Magpie's Rest with her. Mrs Whittington boiled the kettle and served tea and pudding to Gerty, Doris, Mildred and me on the front veranda while the sun set.

As I walked back to our house, Mrs Whittington yelled out, 'If you find young Blue, tell her I've been looking for her!'

Monday, 23 April

Cassie got hysterical at recess. She was walking around sobbing, carrying her banana. It was too tough to peel.

The Colonel sat her down on the veranda and brought her a glass of water. Then he pulled a piece of fishing line from his shorts pocket, made it into a little noose, slipped it over the banana, gave a sudden tug and off flew the end of the skin. He peeled the sides down and handed the banana back to Cassie.

Cassie was astonished. She stared at the Colonel and whispered, 'Thank you, Colonel! You are so clever!'

The rest of the kids were astonished too.

They'd never seen such an odd way to peel bananas. They thought it was cool.

I thought it was stupid. What's wrong with just using a knife to chop off the end, or your teeth? *Miss McKenzie* would be able to peel a banana without making a fuss about it.

Received our first contribution for *The Bake Tribune* today.

Wes and Fez's modern manners

Polite words are really, really important. They make people think you are nice and if you don't use them your mum yells at you.

Always say please, thank you and excuse me, unless there is an emergency.

DO SAY:

Would you please pass the sugar?

Can I please go to the toilet, Mr Cluff?

Thank you for the delicious cake.

Excuse me for making that dreadful smell.

DON'T SAY:

Could you please duck before that rock hits you in the head?

Excuse me, could you please stop that crocodile from chewing off my leg?

Tuesday, 24 April

Good grief! Just about everyone brought a banana and a piece of fishing line to school today. There were chunks of yellow fruit peel flying everywhere. Nick lost control of his banana, and it flew through the air until it collided with the Colonel's head.

The Colonel frowned and said, 'Reminds me of the Great Fruit Fight on Mount Fuji back in 1978. Jolly well nearly drowned in orange juice ... black eye from an apple ... slipped on a banana peel and ended up with a spiky pineapple stuck in a very uncomfortable spot. Dangerous, dangerous times. Still, it was worth it. I was awarded the Purple Plum for bravery. A great honour!'

His eyebrows wriggled like two hairy caterpillars crawling across his forehead, and he walked away.

Nick Farrel and Gary Hartley burst out laughing, but Harry Wilson's eyes nearly popped out of his head. He spent the rest of the day telling everyone that the Colonel had been awarded

the Purple Plum for bravery in the Battle of the Fruit Salad. By three o'clock, all the little kids were gaping at the Colonel like he was a superhero when really he's a big fat liar.

Miss McKenzie never used to lie …

Wednesday, 25 April

Anzac Day ceremony today. Everyone in Hardbake Plains turned out to honour our local men and women who have served in the armed forces. Worms and Dora nearly burst with pride when they lay the school wreath on the War Memorial. It was beautiful — an enormous ring of eucalyptus leaves, red geraniums and gumnuts.

Harry ran around at the sausage sizzle afterwards checking all the men's medals to see if anyone had a Purple Plum. Old Mr Windsor said he had medals for Tom-Foolery, Scaredy-Pantsery and Knee-Knockery, but he was never heroic enough to win a Purple Plum.

Mr Windsor's name is on a special plaque in the Town Hall for being extremely brave during the Vietnam War. He risked his life to save nine of his mates, but he never talks about it. None of the brave old men do. I think they're just grateful that they came home from the war — not like the ones that have their names on the memorial.

As I stood in the memorial garden, eating my sausage sandwich and keeping a keen journalist's eye on everything, I noticed something disturbing. *Everyone* was making the Colonel feel very welcome. They were all shaking his hand and inviting him to darts at the pub, bush dances at the hall and barbecues at their farms.

What a disaster! If everyone accepts the Colonel into their lives, they won't want him to leave. And if he doesn't leave, there's no need for Miss McKenzie to rush back to us.

So I have devised a plan.

I AM GOING TO GET RID OF THE COLONEL.

Plotting and scheming to get rid of a teacher ... now *there's* something new for me to experience!

Emailed Miss McKenzie this afternoon. Told her how special the Anzac ceremony was and how much she would have loved it. Let her know that Mr Cluff is pretty much useless since she left, and Mrs Whittington is completely lost without her. Also hinted that the Colonel probably wouldn't be here for long.

Just preparing the way for her return ...

Thursday, 26 April

The Colonel has gone nuts. It's disturbing, but at least it will make it easier to get rid of him.

He lined his junior class up like an army regiment this morning. He made them stand to attention outside for *ten minutes* while he lectured them on being good little soldiers. Poor things.

Mat, Ben and I spied on them through the window of our study room.

The Colonel boomed on about shiny shoes, clean fingernails, fresh handkerchiefs and faces scrubbed until the cheeks glowed. He lectured them about the evils of wrinkled shirts and the benefits of orderly hair. Then he marched them around the boundary of the schoolyard *three times*.

The little kids must have been scared out of their wits ... and tired! I was expecting Dora or Cassie, the kindy girls, to dissolve into tears at any moment. But they were all very brave and put up with it. They stuck their little chests out and marched like machines.

Spent all of lunch time worm whispering in the compost heap with Sam, Lynette and Lucy. We were up to our necks in rotting vegies and rabbit poo, but it was fun. The worms are really quite cute!

15

Friday, 27 April

The little kids all turned up at school today looking like they had scrubbed and polished themselves for hours. It's the first time Harry Wilson's knees haven't been caked in mud since he started school last year, and it just didn't look right. Ned Murphy had parted his hair at the side and slicked it down with oil. Dora had a big, blue satin bow sticky taped to her crew cut.

The minute the bell rang at nine o'clock, the whole junior class lined up near the flagpole and stood to attention. They must be terrified of the Colonel. Harry stuck his shoulders back, chin up and chest out so far that he fell over backwards.

The Colonel inspected ears, nostrils, fingernails, shoes, hair and handkerchiefs and bellowed out how proud he was to see such a shining group of soldiers.

Mr Cluff's senior students straggled inside looking like a mob of disorderly sheep. Mr Cluff is a sack of misery who can't even be bothered to comb his *own* hair, let alone get enthusiastic about his students' appearance. He's pining for Miss McKenzie.

Which is worse? A crazy Colonel who turns the students into an army of terrified little soldiers, or a misery-guts who doesn't even seem to notice that his students exist? We *really* need Miss McKenzie back soon.

Received two contributions for *The Bake Tribune* today. One was a story about a fairy, a kitten and two ponies from Grace Simpson. It's called 'A Fairy, a Kitten and Two Ponies'. The other was an unusual article about fruit from Ned:

Fruit

People like fruit.

Fruit is yummy and it is good for you.

But many people don't realise that fruit can be dangerous.

Is there anything funny or delicious about a prickly pineapple in an uncomfortable spot?

I don't think so.

Next time you eat an apple, treat it with respect.

Showed Mr Cluff so that he could see the ridiculous stuff the Colonel is teaching the little kids. He just stared into the distance and sighed, 'Miss McKenzie loves apples.'

HELP!!!

Saturday, 28 April

Woken at 4 am by Macka the alpaca's squealing. Two foxes were hanging around the chicken coop. We shooed them away, but it's only a matter of time before they sneak past Macka and steal the chooks. After all, they managed to get Gunther's poor ducks.

Wes and Fez are furious. They still cry when they think about the ducks being killed.

'Stinkin' foxes,' said Wes. 'We'll teach them a lesson.'

'Yeah,' said Fez. 'And we don't mean six plus six equals fourteen!'

Good grief.

They spent the rest of the day making a pit trap near the chicken coop. They dug a deep hole and covered it with sticks, bark and leaves so it was invisible.

Hope it works. I hate foxes.

Sunday, 29 April

Wes and Fez got up at 3 am and climbed onto the laundry roof to watch their pit trap in action.

The foxes didn't turn up. Wes fell asleep and rolled off the roof into a blackberry bush. He cried so loudly that he probably scared off every single fox this side of the Black Stump.

Mrs Whittington disappeared today. We found her wandering around three paddocks away. She said she was going to help Dad shear the sheep, but Dad was way off in the opposite direction sowing canola. Gertrude, Mildred and Doris were with her and looked quite relieved to see us. I think they realise that Mrs Whittington should be at home where she is safe.

Monday, 30 April

The juniors marched around the edge of the schoolyard *four times* this morning. Worms was so hungry by the time they got into class that we could hear his tummy rumbling from our year seven study room. He ate all of his morning tea and lunch at recess — two bananas, three lamingtons, a tub of yoghurt, two cheese salad sandwiches, a boiled egg and a bottle of chocolate milk.

Mr Cluff had to ring Mrs Love to bring some more food in for his lunch. Worms gets very emotional if he doesn't get enough to eat.

Had our first whole-school outdoor adventure lesson this afternoon. We were disappointed when the Colonel said we were going to learn basic first aid. Everyone was hoping for abseiling or archery or something really action-packed.

Instead we learnt about bandaging and splinting, stretcher making, fever, exposure to heat and cold, and treating shock. Halfway into the lesson, Gabby was convinced that she was now an expert on diagnosing fever and disease. She started recording everyone's pulse rate in her maths book and sent three kids and Petal to the sick bay. Jack Scott and Davo Hartley disappeared into the state forest looking for snakes so we could get some real-life practice treating snakebites. Sam ran around in the twenty-five degree heat, herding everyone together and yelling, 'Huddle up for warmth. Use your combined body heat. We don't want to get hypothermia!'

Ned Murphy ended up bandaged from neck to toe, with both arms and legs in splints. Gary and Nick tried to bring him down the steps of the veranda with a special four-handed seat carry, but dropped him down instead. Ned's forehead split open and bled heaps, despite the fact that Grace Simpson ran round and round in circles, yelling, 'Apply pressure! Apply pressure!'

Banjo sat nearby, working through some lines for his next poem, 'Ode to a Complex Accident'. I heard him mutter, 'Bleeding head … nearly dead … bones shattered … guts splattered …'

It's a good thing the Colonel knows so much about first aid, because he had a pretty bad case of shock himself by the end of the lesson. Hee hee!

Wes and Fez spent the evening cutting up their blankets and sewing them to Mum's mop and broom handles. They now have four stretchers to use in an emergency.

When it was time for bed, Fez started crying because they didn't have enough blankets. He was worried they'd die of hypothermia in the night. He tried cuddling up to Wes for body warmth but Wes called him a sissy pink-pants and punched him in the nose.

May

Tuesday, 1 May

The pit trap worked. It must have been totally camouflaged because Mum fell down it at 7 am and sprained her ankle.

Wes and Fez put all their first aid learning straight into action.

'Don't worry, Mummy Darling Heart,' Fez yelled.

'Doctor Wes and Nursey Fez are coming to the rescue!' Wes yelled.

I think that might be when she really started to panic.

They grabbed one of their blanket and broomstick stretchers and carried Mum over to the veranda, where they dropped her on top of Fluffles. Now Mum has a sprained ankle *and* three cat scratches down her left arm. Fluffles has a broken tail.

Wes and Fez offered to bandage Mum up but she said they'd already done enough, thank you very much! They splinted and bandaged Fluffles instead. Poor cat can hardly walk her tail is so stiff and heavy. She looks like a feather duster.

Explained to Mum that none of this would have happened if the Colonel hadn't filled Wes and Fez's heads with crazy ideas.

Gabby turned up at school with a red clipboard, a thermometer and a first aid kit. She was dead jealous when Wes and Fez told her all about their real-life emergency this morning, so she spent the whole of recess doing check-ups on the juniors and sending them into the sick bay. She was terribly upset when Mr Cluff sent them back into class for maths.

Mat, Ben and I have decided that the first edition of *The Bake Tribune* should come out next Friday. I already have two news items. 'Boy eats twelve sausage sandwiches' by Davo Hartley is a riveting story about Worms's day out at the Anzac barbecue. 'Spinach leaf shaped like Madagascar' by Sam Wotherspoon tells of the amazing discovery made in his vegie patch last week. Of course, *all* spinach leaves are shaped like Madagascar because Madagascar is shaped like a spinach leaf, but hopefully our readers won't realise this.

Wednesday, 2 May

Gabby gave me an article for the newspaper today. She said it's important that the whole community knows how to treat emergencies as well as she does.

First aid essentials

Every home should have a first aid kit. First aid kits can be expensive and bothersome to put together, but if they save just one life they are worth it.

These are the things a good first aid kit needs:

1. A thermometer — for taking temperatures. If a patient's temperature is 100°C this means they have reached boiling point and will be very hot. If it is 0°C they will be freezing.
2. Five bandages — one for each arm and leg and one for the head, just in case of a very exciting accident like somersaulting down the stairs.

3. A stopwatch — to time how long it takes for the ambulance to arrive.

4. A snake — many people do not realise that antivenin is made from snake venom. If someone is bitten by a snake you can just get the first aid snake to bite them again and everything will be hunky-dory.

5. A sharp knife — for amputations.

6. Little triangle sandwiches — like they give you in hospital. These are for eating when you are hungry.

7. Clean underwear — for when people get a dreadful fright.

There are many other useful things you can include in your first aid kit, like sticking plaster, scissors and wound dressings, but these are the main ones.

I showed Gabby's article to the Colonel so he could see what a disaster his first outdoor education lesson has been. But he just wriggled his bushy

eyebrows up and down like two feral furry caterpillars and said, 'By gum, that's a *fascinating* list of first aid essentials,' and walked away whistling!

Maybe he won't be so excited when it goes in *The Bake Tribune* and everyone in the community reads it. He won't seem so clever and charming then, will he?

Mat has spent hours staring at a blank computer screen today. She is meant to be writing part one of her romance serial. I told her Petal could type faster than her, but she said real romance needs time to blossom.

Whatever.

Thursday, 3 May

Sarah got hysterical this morning just before the school bell rang. Her scissors were jammed open and she was worried about them being dangerous. Sarah's the Hardbake Plains Scissors Police. She's always telling kids not to run with scissors and to pass them to someone else handles first.

The Colonel sat her down on the steps and removed the scissors from her hand. He took a tiny tin from his pocket, removed a blob of butter and rubbed it up and down the blades until they could open and close smoothly.

Sarah was amazed, although quite concerned at how close the Colonel had come to chopping his fingers off. Some kids are easily impressed, that's for sure!

Banjo handed in a poem for the newspaper today:

Ode to a Complex Accident

A man fell down the slippery stairs
And crashed into a pile of chairs.
So much blood poured from his nose
It spurted like a garden hose.
He tried to stand but staggered round
And landed back onto the ground.
His lips were bruised, his bones were shattered.
His guts were torn and totally splattered.
His spleen exploded, his legs fell off.
He also had a dreadful cough.
His eyes rolled back into his head
And then he was extremely dead.
The moral of the tale, you see,
Is walk down steps real carefully.

Let Mat give me a manicure at lunch time, just to experience something new … and because she nagged the guts out of me. My fingernails are now slime green (although Mat calls it 'Meadow Glisten'). It looks like I have gangrene. Hope Gabby doesn't see or she'll want to amputate my hands!

Petal keeps nibbling hungrily at my fingertips. She must think they are pond slime or tiny green froglets.

Friday, 4 May

Half the kids brought little jars and plastic containers of butter to school in their pockets today. By recess, every pair of scissors and every zipper in the junior room was smeared with a thick layer of butter. It smelt like a CWA scone baking competition.

At recess, Worms got his tongue caught in the zip of his pencil case when he tried to lick the butter off. Gabby dragged him over to the shade and was recording his pulse when Wes and Fez ran over to help. They bandaged Worms's right leg and put his left arm in a sling.

Gabby was furious. She said Worms was *her* patient and they were interfering. Wes shoved Gabby and Gabby shoved Fez. Fez fell over on the edge of Gabby's first aid box and cut his forehead. Worms went into shock at the sight of all the blood dripping off Fez's face, vomited and fainted.

Gabby ran into the girls' toilets, crying. Just when she was really needed!

I wandered over to Mr Cluff and pointed out that none of this would have happened if the Colonel hadn't buttered Sarah's scissors in the first place.

Mr Cluff just sighed and said, 'Miss McKenzie loves butter cake. She used to bring me a slice to have with my cuppa every now and then. Delicious …'

He keeps focusing on the WRONG THING!

Butter Cake McKenzie emailed tonight. She hadn't replied earlier because she'd been hiking up in the mountains for two weeks, trying to find herself (Huh??). I replied that she was welcome to hike around the paddocks at Hillrose Poo any time she liked. The crops will soon be sprouting and the paddocks will be as green as lime cordial. It will be the most beautiful place on earth.

Saturday, 5 May

Woken by Macka squealing at the foxes at 4 am. Wes ran out past the chicken coop, waving a shovel at them and fell down the pit trap. The shovel flipped up and hit him right between the eyes.

Dad ran over to help, but Wes thought he was a fox running through the dark. He grabbed the shovel, swung it up and whacked Dad across the shins. Wes bawled his eyes out in the ditch and Dad hopped around in the dark cursing. Macka stopped squealing and ran around them in circles gurgling with joy.

Wes spent all day sleeping.

Fez and I spent all afternoon running around with undies on our heads, throwing sultanas at Gunther until he chased us up the peppercorn tree.

It's not something I'd normally choose to do, but I have to admit, it was really fun. Especially when Gunther caught Fez and ripped the seat out of his pants!

Sunday, 6 May

Wes fainted during one of the prayers in Mass today. Gabby was right there beside him in a flash, sticking her thermometer under his tongue. Halfway through the sermon she yelled out in her most important voice, 'Praise the Lord! He's going to live!'

Mat spent the entire sermon scribbling notes for her romance serial in the front of the hymn book. Father O'Malley thought she was taking notes on his sermon and kept giving her encouraging looks as he spoke.

After Mass, Mat said she will have the most romantic story ever for our first edition of the newspaper. She said it will make my heart flutter and my knees turn to jelly. If it's anything like the romances Sophie reads, it will make my *lunch* flutter in my stomach and my *brain* turn to jelly. I hope it isn't too embarrassing!

Mrs Whittington sat in the garden with Gunther and his bunnies all afternoon, knitting and chatting. The bunnies played with the balls of wool. Gunther lay nearby and made a sneezing noise which I think is pig laughter.

When Mrs Whittington came over for dinner, she gave Wes and Fez a new orange and green striped tea cosy each. She told them not to eat them all at once or they might get a tummy ache.

Monday, 7 May

Had our second outdoor adventure lesson today. It was on ropes. The Colonel had a whole heap of harnesses, climbing helmets and ropes that he set up around the school. By the end of the day everyone had learnt to winch themselves to the top of the monkey bars, walk up and down the boys' toilet wall and swing themselves across the sandpit.

It was fantastic fun, but there was no way that I was going to admit it. I tried to look totally unimpressed all afternoon. I rolled my eyes, frowned and threw withering looks at the Colonel, but Mr Cluff just thought I had a tummy ache and made me lie down on the veranda. Gabby started taking my temperature every five minutes and explained that I probably had wind and would feel better if I could let it all out!

It was a big fat disaster. *I* missed out on half the activities, while everyone else had loads of fun. Even Mat enjoyed it, although she was quite concerned that the harness made her bum look big. It did, but I couldn't tell her because Gabby's thermometer was stuffed in my mouth. Very disappointing!

As soon as we got home, Wes and Fez used Dad's ropes to climb up to the top of the peppercorn tree. They couldn't get down again. Dad had to ring the Bush Fire Brigade to come out with their truck that has the long fire ladder on the back. The CWA women always go wherever the Fire Brigade goes, just in case they need food. Gabby came out with her mum just in case someone needed a leg amputated. Worms came out with his granny just in case there were extra scones or lemon meringue pies to be eaten.

By the time Wes and Fez were rescued, Mum had eighteen guests for dinner. Dad and Mr O'Donnell cooked a barbecue. Mum and the CWA served up mountains of apple crumble, ice cream and custard. Gabby ran around with blankets in case anybody got hypothermia from eating too much ice cream.

Before everyone went home, I stood up on the veranda and said that I had an important announcement to make. I frowned and began, 'It's thanks to the Colonel that you all had to come out here tonight. He's the one who taught Wes and Fez to use ropes for climbing.'

I was about to point out that the Colonel was not a suitable teacher for our school, but I was rudely interrupted. Mr Sweeney raised his glass of lemonade and yelled, 'To the Colonel!'

Everyone else cheered and toasted the Colonel. They laughed and said what a fabulous, fun night it had been, *thanks to the Colonel!!!*

Talk about backfiring!

My plan is not working.

Tuesday, 8 May

Received three separate articles for the paper about last night's events. 'Rescued treasure' by Mrs Flanagan tells the heartwarming story of how Bert Hartley discovered her long-lost recipe for apple turnovers in the pocket of his Bush Fire Brigade overalls. 'Close shave' by Ted Riley describes how he nearly hit an emu with the fire truck on the way out to Hillrose Poo. 'Shocking experience' by Gabby tells how Worms needed to be treated for shock when he realised that all the apple crumble had run out before he could go back for seconds last night.

No-one even mentions Wes and Fez. They forgot all about them. Wish I could do the same ...

After lunch, the juniors showed us the latest parade they have been practising. They marched around the yard as they echoed the Colonel's chant:

I don't know what you've been told
I don't know what you've been told
Wax in ears can lead to mould
Wax in ears can lead to mould
Dirty hankies spread disease
Dirty hankies spread disease
Just like mud and blood on knees
Just like mud and blood on knees
Shine your shoes and comb your hair
Shine your shoes and comb your hair
And always wear clean underwear
And always wear clean underwear

Everyone clapped and cheered. Except me, of course. I tried to look *totally* unimpressed while being careful not to appear as if I had stomach ache. It was quite difficult but I think I pulled it off.

Wes and Fez fixed up their pit trap this afternoon. As they worked they sang their own special little ditty. Fez sang and Wes repeated the words:

Foxes are real mean and dumb
Foxes are real mean and dumb
They deserve a boot up the bum
They deserve a boot up the bum

They staggered around laughing so much that Fez fell down the pit and grazed his chin.

Twits!

Wednesday, 9 May

Woken by Macka squealing and chasing the foxes at 5 am. Just got back to sleep and we were woken by  Gertrude squealing because she had fallen down the pit trap. Dad had to winch her out using the tractor.

The classifieds section of our paper is looking quite impressive. I have three items:

COMMUNITY NOTICE

The weekly meeting of the Cheese Tasters' Club will not take place this month due to the unfortunate loss of President Barry Scott's false teeth.

FREE TO GOOD HOME

Betty
Kind, smart blue heeler
Buries bones in the bed
Ring Agnes Williams

WANTED

Brown snake
Must be in good health and
able to fit in a standard-sized
first aid kit.
See Gabby

Tom gave me his first survey. The idea is for everyone to complete and return it so that Tom can publish the findings in the next edition of the newspaper.

What is your favourite fruit?

- ❏ apples
- ❏ bananas
- ❏ oranges
- ❏ chocolate
- ❏ pineapple
- ❏ grapes
- ❏ peaches

Good grief! At least no-one other than Tom will be dumb enough to choose chocolate.

Matilda Jane the Mature has been spending a lot of time at her computer sighing, rolling her eyes, clutching her chest and fluttering her eyelashes. I just hope she is actually *writing* something for her romance serial. The paper comes out in two days!

Thursday, 10 May

Mr Cluff gave me an article for *The Bake Tribune* today.

'Soldiers, prepare for bivouac!' announces that the Colonel and Mr Cluff will be taking the whole school on a good old-fashioned rough and tumble camping trip in the second week of next term. Gumbledong Ridge near the Warrumbungles is the perfect site with a creek, thick bushland, wild goats, rocks and cliffs. The rest of the term will be spent teaching students adventure and survival skills. Students should be prepared for action!

Everyone will be so excited when they read this.

I'm excited and I don't even want the Colonel to stay! A camp is a brilliant idea.

Bummer!

I think I'll try to bury the article deep in the

paper where no-one will see it — maybe in small print at the end of old Mr Grange's three-page essay on the joys of stamp collecting. No need to make the Colonel seem more exciting than he really is.

Mrs Whittington's report, 'School bus hit by meteorite', will be the newspaper's lead story. It's a sensational article describing a tragic meteorite storm that occurred in Hardbake Plains last Tuesday. In addition to the school bus being blasted into a crater the size of Mount Vesuvius, the pub, the church and Wes and Fez were completely annihilated.

None of it is real, of course. Mrs Whittington gets a bit confused sometimes. She watched a movie called *The End* with Wes and Fez last Sunday night, and has mixed the details up with real life in Hardbake Plains.

Our readers won't mind. They'll be happy for Mrs W that her story made the front page.

Friday, 11 May

A newspaper is born!

The first ever edition of *The Bake Tribulation* came out today. Of course, it was meant to be *The Bake Tribune*, but Ben made a printing error.

A tribulation is a dreadful, traumatic experience, so, really, it might be a more accurate name for our poor readers. Especially when they see Mat's romance serial …

Heart's Triumph

Elizabeth, a tall, slender woman of overwhelming beauty, walked down the curved staircase into the chandelier-lit ballroom. Her heart fluttered violently as she looked across the crowded room and saw a tall, slender man of overwhelming handsomeness. He turned around from the table loaded with caviar and lobsters and his heart fluttered violently as he looked across the room and saw Elizabeth.

'Who is that tall, slender woman of overwhelming beauty?' he asked Lady Welsh-Pearson.

Lady Welsh-Pearson sneered, 'She is nobody. Don't waste your time with the likes of her, Edmund. She is only the butcher's daughter.'

But it was too late. It was love at first sight. Edmund was like totally in love with her forever.

He rushed across the room, seized Elizabeth by the hand and dragged her out onto the balcony.

'Oh dear lady,' Edmund cried. 'You are totally awesome. Your hair is like black silk. Your skin is like pure snow. Your eyes are like blue poo

Unfortunately, Ben's dodgy printing cut the last bit off. Mat will be hysterical when she reads it.

Wes and Fez cried when they learnt that they'd been killed in a meteorite storm last Tuesday …

Saturday, 12 May

Had heaps of phone calls from people telling me how much they *loved* the newspaper. Mrs Murphy said she hadn't laughed so much since Mr Murphy fell down the chute in the shearing shed last year. She thought it was pure gold from cover to cover.

The crazy fruit and first aid articles have been an enormous hit, and everyone is busting with excitement about the camp. It's not going to be easy to turn people against the Colonel.

Mat rang in tears.

'Ben ruined my romance,' she cried. 'Edmund was meant to tell Elizabeth her eyes are like blue *pools*, but now everyone will think her eyes are like blue *poo!*'

I told her nobody would even notice (BIG LIE!!!). But she blabbered on and on and sobbed so hard that she sounded like a camel with a fig stuck in its throat.

Gross.

But not as gross as having eyes like blue poo!

Sunday, 13 May

Mat rang again today. Her nose was so blocked up, she must have been crying for hours.

It turns out that she had scanned and emailed a copy of *The Bake Tribulation* to Warren from Warren on Friday afternoon before reading it. Warren now thinks Mat has a disgusting obsession with bottoms and poo. He emailed today to say that he doesn't want to be her boyfriend any more.

Poor Mat. Romance is never easy.

Mrs Whittington gave Wes and Fez a khaki tea cosy each today.

She said, 'Don't eat them all at once or you'll get a tummy ache.'

She must have forgotten that she has just given them the orange and green striped ones.

Wes and Fez are really excited.

'Cool as,' cried Wes.

'Army tea cosies!' cried Fez.

'These are just like real soldiers wear!' cried Wes.

They spent the whole evening marching up and down the veranda with their tea cosies on their heads, yelling, 'Left–right–left–right!' even though they don't know their right from their left.

Monday, 14 May

Everyone was talking about blue poo on the bus this morning.

Nick said his poo turned blue once after eating bubble gum-flavoured ice cream. Grace wondered if blueberries would turn your poo blue, but Worms said he had eaten two jars of blueberry jam just the other day and everything was normal. Jack's dog had eaten all the blue tinsel off their Christmas tree one year and his poo was full of glittery blue bits, but everyone agreed that it didn't really count.

Mat sat up the front seething. You could almost see the steam coming out her ears.

Wes and Fez wore their khaki tea cosies to school today.

The Colonel was impressed.

'Interesting pieces of headwear,' he said. 'Very creative! Very creative! Reminds me of the Ice Tribes of Siberia who wear live snow foxes on their heads for warmth. Tried it myself once when I was lost in a blizzard for three days.

Astonishingly warm with all that fur and body heat … Of course, the foxes don't like it much, but they adapt.'

I rolled my eyes and tried to look bored, but in the end I had to run into the toilets to hide the grin that was splitting my face. Gabby thought I had wind issues again and spent all day begging me to lie down in the sick bay!

Posted three copies of *The Bake Tribulation* today — one to Sophie, one to Peter and one to Miss McKenzie in Scotland.

Haven't heard from Miss McKenzie for over a week. I hope she hasn't disappeared into the mountains for good. What will we do if she never comes back?

What will Mr Cluff do if she never comes back? He can't go on moping around like a blob for the rest of his life, can he?

My plan just has to work.

Tuesday, 15 May

Harry Wilson came to school with his face covered in scratches. Apparently he got cold during the night and thought it would be a good idea to use his pet rabbit as a hat. The rabbit obviously didn't agree.

I told Harry's mum that the Colonel has been putting crazy ideas into Harry's head. She said Harry's head is already stuffed so full of crazy ideas, like digging to China and hot air ballooning to Greenland, that a few more crazy ideas wouldn't make a jot of difference. Besides, what were a few scratches when Harry's knees and face were the cleanest they'd ever been since he could crawl, all thanks to the Colonel?

Darn it! Foiled again.

Today's outdoor adventure activity was archery. I tried to look like it was a total yawn, but it was so much fun that I don't think I got my point across. I was the best in the school with seventeen bull's-eyes and heaps more *just* missing.

Sam was pretty upset because Ben accidentally shot his giant pumpkin that was almost ready to be picked.

Mat refused to participate in archery. She sat on the veranda steps, pushing her hair behind her ears, and jotting down ideas for part two of 'Heart's Triumph'. She is determined to make it so beautifully romantic that Warren from Warren will be speechless and will apologise for his heartless treatment of her and declare his undying love. I said that was an awful lot to say for someone who is speechless. Mat just gave me one of her withering looks and started drawing little love hearts down her fingers with red pen.

Dad was pretty excited when we told him about the archery. He was Senior Boys' Champion in archery at boarding school and still has his bow and arrows somewhere in the shed. He promised to find them for us tomorrow. Mum just rolled her eyes.

Wednesday, 16 May

Received a news article from Sam for the next edition of *The Bake Tribulation*. 'Murderer roams free' is a bloodthirsty account of the slaughter of Sam's pumpkin during yesterday's archery lesson.

Also got a moving poem from Banjo:

A Sudden Loss
A pumpkin - orange, large and plump
Sitting in the soil,
A product of Sam's love and care
And horse manure and toil.
An arrow - long and thin and sharp

Flying swift and true.
The skin is pierced, the pumpkin's dead.
Oh what is Sam to do?

I showed them both to the Colonel so that he would realise how much destruction and heartache he'd been responsible for in one short lesson. He wriggled his bushy eyebrows and said, 'Golly gosh and galloping grapes! That young Ben is a *killer* shot with an arrow ... Quite impressive ... Quite impressive,' and walked away humming a tune.

I read the article to Mr Cluff, so that he would realise how out of control the Colonel's lesson had been. But he just stared out across the plains and sighed, 'Miss McKenzie's hair is the colour of pumpkin soup.'

SOMEBODY HELP ME!!!

Showed the article and poem to Ben and he just shrugged his shoulders. He didn't seem at all ashamed of himself. I hope he isn't a psychopath.

Wes, Fez and I spent all evening practising archery with Dad's old bow and arrows so we can shoot the foxes next time they come sneaking around. One of Fez's arrows landed in the grass right next to Gunther and his bunnies. Gunther was furious and chased Fez around the chicken coop where he fell down the pit trap and gave himself a bleeding nose.

Macka appeared from nowhere and ran around the pit gurgling happily.

Thursday, 17 May

Ned could hardly wait to sit down on the school bus this morning before he shared his fascinating news. Yesterday his baby sister had sucked on the blue crepe paper streamers they used to decorate the kitchen for his mum's birthday, and first thing today … drum roll … her nappy was full of blue poo!!

The whole bus exploded in cheers.

Mat burst into tears. She really needs to develop a sense of humour.

This afternoon, the Colonel gathered us all together and said, 'I've got one word for you — carrier pigeons.'

I rolled my eyes and said, 'That's *two* words!'

The Colonel's hairy eyebrows wriggled across his forehead and he said, 'By Jove it is! And two very important words. Can't get enough of carrier pigeons. Astonishing creatures! Useful for sending messages between soldiers. Brilliant for getting SOS signals back to base when trouble strikes.'

Tom suggested using mobile phones or walkie-talkies, but the Colonel frowned and said, 'Now where's the fun in that?'

He's right. Pigeons sound like much more fun. I wish he would stop making everything so exciting.

The Colonel told us that carrier pigeons have something called magnetite in their brains. It works like a compass that draws on the earth's magnetic field. So even when a carrier pigeon is taken miles away from home, it still knows how to get back. That makes it very handy for sending messages home to family and friends.

Anyway, we are expecting eight carrier pigeons to be delivered to Hardbake Plains Public School on Monday. I asked Davo and Jack to write an article about carrier pigeons for the next edition of *The Bake Tribulation*. They're sure to write something dodgy that I can then blame on the Colonel ...

Friday, 18 May
Have two more news articles ready for the next edition of *The Bake Tribulation*. 'Sink your teeth

into cheese' by Edna Scott is proof that our newspaper is a great thing for Hardbake Plains. Thanks to the generous donation of *three* pairs of false teeth, President Barry Scott is now able to chair this month's meeting of the Cheese Tasters' Club.

'Blueberries — the naked truth' by Davo Hartley sheds new light on the whole blue poo issue. Apparently *fresh* blueberries can have quite a different effect to blueberry jam! There are some interesting descriptions from Davo's cousin Marianne, whose parents own a berry farm near Armidale.

Worms was getting very emotional at recess because he couldn't open his third muesli bar. The Colonel pulled a magnifying glass from his pocket, lined it up between the sun and the muesli bar and held it there until a beam of light burnt through the end of the wrapping. He blew the ashes away, tore the hole open, pulled out the muesli bar and handed it to Worms.

Worms was so grateful, he nearly fainted.

I pointed out to Mat (at the top of my voice, so that everyone in the playground could hear) that scissors would have worked much faster. It backfired because Sarah spent the rest of recess lecturing me on the dangers of bringing *naked* scissors out into the playground where children were running and galloping and leaping and could end up impaled on the end of a sharp blade!

Found Mrs Whittington asleep in her chicken coop behind Magpie's Rest this afternoon. Macka was sitting outside the fence as though he was keeping guard.

When I woke Mrs Whittington and led her inside, she was very upset because she had missed afternoon tea with Gertrude, Mildred and Doris. Gertrude, Mildred and Doris didn't seem too upset. They had broken into Mrs W's kitchen, had eaten all her jam drops and were sleeping in front of the old wood stove.

Saturday, 19 May

Wes and Fez shot arrows through three towels, two T-shirts, a pillowcase, Mum's pink nighty and a pair of Dad's jocks today. Mum was furious when she took the washing off the line and sent Wes and Fez to their room.

Dad said, 'Oh, well ... I s'pose it could be worse. I could have been *wearing* my jocks at the time.'

He does have a point there.

By the time Wes and Fez came out for dinner, they had burnt their names on their windowsill using a magnifying glass and written their next manners column for the newspaper:

Wes and Fez's modern manners

This week we look at peas. Everyone hates peas but it is rude to say, 'Yuck! I hate peas!' You have to say, 'Yummo! These peas are delicious, thank you, Mummy Darling Heart,' and pretend to eat them.

These are the best ways to get rid of your peas so your mum doesn't think you are being ungrateful when thousands of kids are starving to death in Africa:

1. Hide them in your pockets.
2. Stuff them down your socks.
3. Stuff them down your shorts.
4. Stick them up your nose.
5. Stick them up your brother's nose.
6. Stick them up the cat's nose.
7. Flick them onto your sister's plate.
8. Roll them across the floor until they end up under the china cabinet.

9. Smear them under the seat of your chair.
10. Hide them under your plate (but only do this if you are desperate, because your mum will see them when she clears the table).

Caught them putting numbers 1, 2, 3, 4 and 6 into action at dinner time.

Sunday, 20 May

Woken by foxes at 6.30 am. Wes and Fez ran out with their bows and arrows ready for action. They shot the laundry door five times and smashed three of Mum's pot plants. I wanted a go but they wouldn't let me and the foxes ran free.

Mr Cluff and the Colonel came out to Hillrose Poo today. The Colonel was rapt with the pig chariots. He raced Fez and Mildred along the driveway three times before lunch and won each time!

'Fascinating mode of transport!' he boomed while we ate our roast lamb and gravy. 'Reminds me of the Great Andes Mountain Battle of 1982 where the ambulances ran out of petrol. Had to harness guinea pigs to tow our wounded back to the field hospital. It was a jolly nuisance catching all those little critters ... and darned fiddly weaving those tiny harnesses, but we did it in the end. Saved 457 men in three days, so you can't say it wasn't worth the effort. Fifteen thousand guinea pigs were awarded the Rodent Red Ribbon for Endurance. Amazing feat! I was proud to be a part of it!'

It was very difficult not to laugh. I inhaled three peas trying to suck it all in.

After lunch the Colonel sat on the veranda with Petal and me. Petal popped onto his lap and nibbled affectionately on his shirt buttons. She didn't even poop on him. Little traitor!

'What a magnificent duck!' the Colonel boomed. 'Reminds me of a goose I once had. Wonderful, wonderful pet. Named her Gloria. She could spot a slug on a cabbage from ten metres away and could beat any dog in a fight. Had a nasty habit of hiding all my socks and eating the sultanas out of my cereal. But still, she was a marvellous companion, and was kind-hearted and loyal till the day she died.'

A goose called Gloria! How cute is that?

Why does the Colonel have to be so interesting? And likeable?

I just wish he would go back to the Amazon Jungle or the Himalayan Alps or wherever he comes from, and LEAVE US ALL ALONE.

Monday, 21 May

Woken by foxes at 6.30 am. Wes and Fez ran out with the bow and arrows and shot three veranda posts and a bag of chook pellets. I had a go and shot Dad in the bum as he chased after the foxes with the shovel. Mum has confiscated the archery equipment.

Heaps of kids brought magnifying glasses to school today. They were burning their way through chip packets, sultana boxes and cake wrappings. Gary accidentally set his sandwich wrapping on fire and totally melted his lunchbox. Hope his mum gets mad and blames the Colonel.

Davo and Jack had spent all weekend at Jack's house writing their article on carrier pigeons. It is a truly unique piece of journalism:

Carrier pigeons

Carrier pigeons have special stuff in their brains called magnetite. It is like having a compass or a GPS in their head and shows them how to get home. They don't even need to carry maps.

Carrier pigeons were used in World Wars I and II to send messages between soldiers so they didn't have to run out in front of the enemy just to tell each other when dinner was served or what was on TV. Carrier pigeons were also used to drop bombs on the enemy and carry wounded soldiers back to the hospital.

Nowadays people have carrier pigeons as a hobby. There are competitions where they let the pigeons out a long way from home and they see which one is first to get back home. It's usually the ones that don't get eaten by cats or stop for petrol on the way that win.

The pigeons didn't arrive. It was really disappointing. The Colonel had spent all weekend at school with Mr Cluff and Mr Hartley building a coop, and everyone had been so excited. Maybe they'll come tomorrow.

Tuesday, 22 May

Sunshine had a specials board out the front of the pub when we drove past on the way to school:

> **TODAY'S LUNCH SPECIAL**
> Leek and pigeon pie $12
> Vegetables $5 extra
> Knife and fork $2 extra

I covered Petal's eyes and pointed it out to Banjo, Ben and Mat. Ben said he loved pies. Mat said it was disgusting to charge for a knife and fork. Only Banjo saw the real problem.

Couldn't wait to point the disaster out to the Colonel when we got to school. I thought he would be totally embarrassed and downhearted, but he just wriggled his bushy eyebrows and looked astonished.

'Good heavens!' he cried. 'It's just like the Great Zoological Disaster during the Pacific Crossing of 1978. Ship was filled with exotic animals from the deepest, darkest depths of the Amazon rainforest. Fringe-faced toucans. Ridgebacked sloths. Feathered armadillos. Rainbow alligators. Gold-winged monkeys. Would have made marvellous zoo specimens. But the ship's doctor got hungry and ate them all for a Thanksgiving banquet before we reached New Zealand. Nothing I could do about it of course. Just had to grin and bear it ... Stiff upper lip ... No point getting my knickers in a knot!'

The Colonel disappeared into the office. I suppose he was ordering a new lot of pigeons. He's not easily discouraged!

Had an email from Miss McKenzie this afternoon. She loved *The Bake Tribulation* and said she was very proud of Ben, Mat and me for producing such an amazing newspaper. Her dad, Angus, had laughed so much when he read it that the neighbours came in to see what all the fuss was about. *They* had laughed so much that they had to sit down and have a cup of tea before they could walk home again.

Miss McKenzie said she missed us all heaps and thought of us every day.

If she misses us so much, why doesn't she come back???

Probably because she doesn't think she is needed as long as the Colonel is here!

Showed Mr Cluff her email. He just sighed and rubbed his forehead. At least he didn't talk about pumpkin soup or butter cake!

Wednesday, 23 May

Received three stories for the newspaper today. Two are about four ponies on a picnic and one is about three fairies living with a pony. They are all by Grace Simpson.

Had an outdoor adventure lesson on emergency signals today. SOS stands for 'Save Our Souls', not 'Share Our Sandwiches' as Worms had thought. The Colonel taught us all about Morse code, torch signals, mirrors reflecting sunlight, smoke signals and making big messages out of rocks, logs and clothes. Then we had half an hour to make our own emergency signal.

Mat *just happened* to have a mirror in her pocket. She sat on the steps, flashed SOS in Morse code, then examined her nose and chin for pimples for the rest of the lesson. It must be so boring being mature.

Ben, Banjo, Gabby and I built a fire out of grass, bark and sticks, which gave out heaps of smoke to alert our rescuers. Ben lit it using his magnifying glass — which was very clever but really annoying because it was a Colonel idea.

Cassie and Lucy sat down and wrote a long letter to their mother explaining where she could find them, then went inside for an envelope and stamp. Like *that's* going to be possible when they're lost in the wilderness!

Harry, Ned and Worms made the word HEPL out of their clothes then ran around in their undies. They said anyone flying over was sure to think something was wrong if they saw H-E-P-L and three half-naked boys. Mr Cluff said that you hardly needed to be flying over to think that something was wrong and they better put their clothes back on at once and go inside to practise their spelling.

We were meant to learn about carrier pigeons too, but we'll have to wait until next week ... unless we go to the pub for dinner!

Thursday, 24 May

Received a fascinating article from Ned for the newspaper:

SOS

If you are lost in the bush or floating around in the ocean on a life raft, you need to send out an SOS signal so someone will save you before you starve to death or get eaten by vultures. You need to build a big sign that says SOS using your clothes (but not your undies or you might get sunburnt in uncomfortable places). Once you have made the sign, set fire to it, flash a mirror, have a smoke and throw a pigeon into the air. If that doesn't work, use your mobile phone to ring the emergency services.

Warning: Smoking is a health hazard.

Grace Simpson kept sending me SOS signals using a mirror during her maths test today. She'd forgotten how to do long multiplication and was getting quite upset. I really wanted to help, but Mr Cluff scowled at me every time I tried to creep into the senior classroom.

Mum and Dad were really happy tonight because they got the first big fat cheque for last year's wheat harvest. I know what wheat cheques mean. Wheat cheques mean money in the bank, which means money for boarding school fees, which means GOODBYE BLUE.

The Colonel didn't teach us an SOS signal for getting out of that one, did he?

Friday, 25 May

Woken at 4.30 am by Macka squealing at the foxes. Gunther chased them away before we even woke up properly. He was snorting and frothing at the mouth like a wild dog. Gertrude, Mildred and Doris had formed a ring around Gunther's bunnies so they'd be safe from the foxes.

Eight big fat pigeons arrived at school today. The Colonel said we should leave them alone for the weekend. They need to settle into their new coop before we start training them.

Davo and Jack are really disappointed with how small the pigeons are. Jack said there was no way they'd be able to drop bombs or carry people to safety, so they were as good as useless. Davo said he'd been planning on flying one to his cousin Marianne's to try out the blueberries, but now he'd have to wait.

I said, 'So the Colonel has let you down, huh? Think he's no good, huh? Want him to leave, huh?'

Davo and Jack just stared at me like I was insane. Gabby rushed me into the shade and started treating me for hiccups.

I just can't win.

The pigeons are all brown with white speckles, except for one big black one with feathers all over his feet.

The juniors got to name them so now we have Chocky 1, Chocky 2, Chocky 3, Chocky 4, Chocky 5, Chocky 6, Chocky 7 and Flipper.

Talking about chocolate, Tom has given me the results of his favourite fruit survey for next week's *Bake Tribulation*:

What is your favourite fruit?

Thank you to the fifty-four people who replied.
The results are:

5 apples	3 pineapple
12 bananas	8 grapes
7 oranges	5 peaches
14 chocolate	

Most of the kids at school had said chocolate was by far their favourite fruit.

Got a parcel from Scotland this afternoon. There was a tin of shortbread from Miss McKenzie's mum, Glenda, and a letter from Miss McKenzie saying she was about to head off for a six-day camping trip by Loch Lomond.

Why can't she come back here and camp by one of our farm dams for a few weeks? She could swim and yabby and talk to the sheep when they came down to drink. Wes and Fez could even join her for a leeching competition. She'd love it.

Saturday, 26 May

Spent the morning writing a passionate article for the newspaper, called 'Hardbake Plains has everything and more'. I'm quite proud of it really. I wrote that other places have mountains, waterfalls and beaches, but we have beautiful dusty red plains that change to lush green paddocks as the crops rise from the soil. Other places have cafés, nightclubs and award-winning restaurants, but we have a pub that sells cold beer, lemon squash, chocolate milkshakes *and* pigeon pie. Other places have opera, rock concerts and international sporting events, but we have the CWA Christmas party and the Australia Day picnic races where you can ride a camel, a pig, a wheelbarrow or whatever else you like. Other places have presidents, queens and movie stars, but we have kind, happy people who take care of each other.

I'm hoping Miss McKenzie will read it and realise how much she is missing out on back here. I'm also hoping I will be able to put another important article right below it: 'Colonel loses battle — retreats from Hardbake Plains'.

Spent the afternoon with Wes and Fez making boomerangs. They're to save the chickens. The twin tornadoes explained that you throw the boomerang at the fox and kill it. If the boomerang misses, it comes straight back and you can throw it again. Easy as!

Yeah, right.

Sunday, 27 May

Woken at 5.30 am by Gunther chasing the foxes. Ran out with Wes and Fez and our boomerangs, but we all hit Gunther by mistake. He stopped running after the foxes and chased us up the peppercorn tree. He was not a happy pig.

Went outside after breakfast to practise boomerang throwing. I was going to throw mine from the back veranda out towards the paddock, but Wes and Fez wouldn't let me.

'Boomerangs come back, Blue,' said Wes.

'It'll come back and smash through the dining-room window,' said Fez.

'Mum would get cross,' said Wes.

So we walked down to the back fence. Fez threw his boomerang up towards the house, straight through the kitchen window.

Mum *was* cross. She used the boomerangs to start the log fire in the lounge room. She sent Wes and Fez off in their pig chariots to take Dad a Thermos of tea.

Monday, 28 May

The Colonel gave us the first carrier pigeon lesson today. We have to feed them well and be really kind and gentle. Then they will be happy and always want to return to their home.

The first time you let the pigeons out you just open the coop so they can stretch their wings and find their way back easily. Then, gradually, you take them further and further from their coop, until they can find their way home from hundreds of kilometres away.

We all stood quietly while the Colonel opened the coop and let Chocky 1, Chocky 2, Chocky 3, Chocky 4, Chocky 5, Chocky 6, Chocky 7 and Flipper find their way out. All the Chockies flew straight up into the air and we cheered and clapped. But suddenly, one of them started to somersault backwards and tumble down towards the earth.

Cassie, Lucy and Dora screamed and covered their faces, but it recovered before it crashed and flew back up into the air. It had just reached the other pigeons when they *all* started tumbling backwards, plummeting down towards the ground.

'Engine failure!' yelled Nick.

'Hit the deck!' yelled Davo.

Kids were screaming and running all over the place, as though a squadron of fighter planes was attacking. But the next time we looked, the pigeons were flying back up into the air!

They soared up and tumbled down over and over again. Finally they'd had enough and flew onto the roof of the pigeon coop. One by one, they made their way back inside.

All except for Flipper, that is.

Just when the whole thing was over, Flipper waddled out of the coop, fluffed up his feathers and tumbled ALONG THE GROUND all the way to Sam's vegie patch. He stood up, cooed a few times and tumbled all the way back. He waddled inside the coop and sat down on the ground.

What a crack-up! We staggered around laughing until we got the hiccups. Lynette Sweeney laughed so much that she wet her pants. Even Mr Cluff laughed, and he hasn't cracked a smile since Miss McKenzie left.

The Colonel stared at us, his bushy eyebrows wriggling up and down, and said, 'By hook or by crook, they've sent us the wrong birds! These are Birmingham Rollers, not carrier pigeons.'

And he went into the office to phone for a *third* order of pigeons!

I really *really* wanted to point out that the Colonel had botched it all up *yet again*. But it was all so much fun. I just couldn't do it.

We spent the rest of the afternoon tumbling all over the playground. Grace rolled into Sam's compost heap and lost her headband among the rotting fruit and worms. Harry somersaulted through some wattle bushes and lost his shorts.

The senior boys had a tumbling race along the length of the soccer field. They were so dizzy when they finished that Jack staggered into Tom and accidentally bit his forehead. Davo wobbled into the soccer goal and split his head open. Ben fell over on top of Wes and winded him. Gabby was beside herself with joy as she ran around treating students for shock, cuts and tummy ache from laughing so much.

Nick Farrel can tumble so fast when he somersaults backwards that everyone has started calling him Rolly Farrel. Mr Cluff has always said that each of us has something we can be brilliant at. Nick has found his strength at last. His parents must be very proud of him.

Tuesday, 29 May

The Bake Tribulation will be out again on Friday. Banjo was so moved by yesterday's events that he has written a *second* poem for this edition:

Tumbling

Tumbling, tumbling, tumbling,
Rolling, rolling, rolling,
Somersaulting, somersaulting, somersaulting,
The joy, the joy, the joy,

Visions spinning past my eyes,
Spinning, spinning, spinning,
Around, around, around,
Dizzy, dizzy, dizzy,
Makes me want to vomit.

Nice!

Mat is determined to create the most astonishing romance *ever* for the next paper and spent the whole day writing. She wouldn't even come outside when Flipper and Nick had a rolling race, and it *really* was impressive.

Flipper won because he attacked Nick when they got to the vegie patch. Nick was still thrashing around in agony when Flipper tumbled back to the coop. Who knew a face full of pigeon pecks could hurt so much?

The Colonel took a little tin from his pocket, pulled out six tiny round sticking plasters and patched them over Nick's wounds. Everyone gathered around, trying to see what else the Colonel had in his useful little tin, but he snapped the lid shut and popped it back in his pocket. Jack reckons he saw a tiny hammer and some nails. Tom said there was a candle stub and three matches. Grace thought there were tea bags and mini Easter eggs. Davo swears he saw a little stick of dynamite. How can I possibly turn people against a bloke who carries tiny tins of dynamite in his pocket? It's just too, too cool.

Wednesday, 30 May

Woken at 5.40 am by Gunther and Macka squealing at the foxes. Wes and Fez ran outside and somersaulted across the garden in their pyjamas, screaming and laughing like maniacs. They scared the foxes, Gunther, Macka, Gertrude, Doris, Mildred and the three rabbits away across the paddocks.

Heaps of kids brought little tins and boxes to school in their pockets today. Everyone wants to keep what they have inside a secret, but I did see Worms eating jelly beans from his tin, and Harry took a little car out of his box that he played with in the sandpit. I think Jack has a frog in his because it keeps croaking.

Thursday, 31 May

Flipper has moved to Hillrose Poo. The new carrier pigeons should arrive at school tomorrow and the Colonel said we needed to make room for them. He sent the Birmingham Rollers home with eight different families. Everyone thought Nick should take Flipper because they have so much in common, but Nick said he doesn't want a psycho pigeon living at his house.

Flipper's living with the chooks. There's no roof on the chicken yard, but he can't fly, so it doesn't matter. Wes, Fez and I spent all afternoon feeding him toast and Vegemite in the chicken coop so he associates his new home with happy memories. Petal is jealous. She waddled into a nesting box to sulk, then wouldn't come out when we left.

I'm really excited about tomorrow's *Bake Tribulation*. I love being an editor. I think our paper represents the true Hardbake Plains.

The classifieds are all ready to go:

WANTED

Worms

Any size

Must have a good appetite.

Will swap for weird-shaped carrots.

See Sam at the school vegie patch.

```
┌─────────────────────────────────┐
│          FOR SALE               │
│                                 │
│  Rooster eggs                   │
│  $3 a dozen                     │
│  See Dora or Harry Wilson       │
└─────────────────────────────────┘
```

```
┌─────────────────────────────────────┐
│              LOST                    │
│                                      │
│  If anyone finds my husband, Harold, │
│  could they please return him at once to │
│          Magpie's Rest?              │
│          Lotty Whittington           │
└─────────────────────────────────────┘
```

```
┌──────────────────────────────────────────┐
│             IN MEMORIUM                   │
│                                           │
│          Gerald Simpson                   │
│          Deeply missed                    │
│ A true friend to all whose lives you touched. │
│       A pillar of the community.          │
│ Never was a hermit crab more dearly loved. │
│     Your family — Grace, Ben, Julia,      │
│            Mum and Dad.                    │
└──────────────────────────────────────────┘
```

Poor Ben and Grace. Ben didn't even say anything when he came to school.

June

Friday, 1 June

An exciting day — eight new carrier pigeons *and* a brand-new edition of *The Bake Tribulation*.

The pigeons are beautiful and have already been named — Blue (because it is white with freckles on its face like me — how rude!!!), Tiny Tim (the fattest one), Blacky, Browny, Greyey, Whitey, Patch and Feathers.

Worms named Feathers. When we asked why, he said, 'Duh! Because it has *feathers*!'

Worms is quite concerned that Feathers might feel the cold because he doesn't have fur like all the other pigeons. We tried to explain that *all* birds have feathers, but his tummy started rumbling. He was too hungry to pay attention.

The second edition of *The Bake Tribulation* is a ripper, although I'm not sure how happy Mat will be when she reads part two of her romance:

'Oh, dear lady,' Edmund cried. 'You are totally awesome. Your hair is like black silk. Your skin is like pure snow. Your eyes are like blue POOLS. I am like totally in love with you!'

'Oh, dear sir,' Elizabeth sighed. 'I am like doubly totally in love with you. And, yet, alas, I do not even know your name.'

'My name is Edmund,' he sighed, 'And I love you more.'

'No, I love you more,' Elizabeth sighed.

'No, I love you more,' Edmund sighed.

'No, I love you more,' Elizabeth sighed.

'No, I love you more,' Edmund sighed.

They kissed and sighed.

But just at that moment, Elizabeth's cruel father, Barry the butcher, walked by.

'Elizabeth!' he yelled. 'Get on home and make my supper, scrub the floors, chop the wood and darn my smelly socks.'

Elizabeth swooned in Edmund's strong, manly, handsome arms. 'I must go, my darling,' she sighed. 'Our love can never be. You are a man of high and mighty realms and I am the daughter of a lowly, cruel, dirty butcher. I am nothing more than a slave.'

Edmund clasped her to his chest. 'That means nothing to me!' he sighed. 'You must know that the very sight of your face makes me want to vomit.'

Elizabeth sighed and went tumbling, tumbling, tumbling, rolling, rolling, rolling, somersaulting, somersaulting, somersaulting, spinning, spinning, spinning *down the street, away from Edmund.*

Ben and his dodgy printing! Looks like Banjo's poem got tangled up with the words of Mat's romance. It's funny how that happens with computers sometimes.

Although I'm not so sure Mat will think it's funny …

Saturday, 2 June

Mat *wasn't* amused.

We went over to the Sweeneys' for tennis and a barbecue lunch today, but I ended up spending all day in Mat's bedroom passing her tissues, and saying lame things like 'There, there' and 'The road to love is never easy'.

'Ben ruined my romance *again*!' Mat cried. 'Edmund was meant to tell Elizabeth that the sight of her face makes his heart soar on angels' wings, not that the sight of her face makes him want to vomit.'

Mat cried so hard that snot was streaming out both her nostrils, and the sight of *her* face made *me* want to vomit!

But a friend is a friend, so I gave her a hug and told her that nobody would even notice. And besides, it was quite impressive that Elizabeth was still able to tumble away merrily down the street after Edmund had been so mean. I thought that showed great strength of character on Elizabeth's part.

Mat gave me a withering stare, burst into tears again, and said the tumbling, rolling, somersaulting, spinning part was the WORST OF ALL.

'Imagine how her long skirt and petticoats and legs would have flown up in the air!' cried Mat.

'She would have flashed her bloomers all over the place!' she sobbed.

'It would have been the most humiliating moment of Elizabeth's life!' she shrieked.

Mat threw herself on her bed and cried and cried and cried.

We ran out of tissues.

By the time I went home at four o'clock, I was exhausted and I hadn't played a single game of tennis. Phew! What an afternoon.

It was a relief to come home and have some tumbling races with Wes, Fez and Flipper. Flipper won six races, I won three, and Fez tumbled down the old pit trap for the foxes. Wes staggered around laughing so much at Fez that he tripped over and fell down the pit on top of Fez.

Sunday, 3 June

We let Flipper out of the chicken coop today and he tumbled backwards across the grass until he collided with Mrs Whittington. She was sweeping the dirt off the driveway, even though the whole thing is made of dirt.

Flipper got cross and started pecking Mrs Whittington on the ankles. Mrs W swung the broom back like a hockey stick and belted Flipper so hard that he tumbled backwards all the way to the veranda. Poor thing.

Will post the next edition of *The Bake Tribulation* to Miss McKenzie tomorrow. I'll also send one of Flipper's feathers and our school photo from last year. Just so she knows what she's missing out on.

Monday, 4 June

Everyone was talking about 'Heart's Triumph' on the bus this morning. Tom and Jack were discussing why Edmund wanted to vomit when he looked at Elizabeth's face. Tom said she must be really ugly. Jack said eyes like blue poo would look gross, *and* they'd stink!

Ned said it was totally cool the way Elizabeth went tumbling away at the end of the story. He thought she might turn out to be a Birmingham Roller, like in those stories where people turn out to be spiders or tigers, take over the earth and eat all the people for vitamins. Nick said Elizabeth would probably peck Edmund and Barry the butcher to death before the serial ended — like a science-fiction blood-and-guts action story. Now everyone is really excited about what will happen in the next episode.

You'd think Mat would be pleased to have written such a popular serial, but she's not. She sat up the front of the bus, blowing her nose and pretending not to hear. Then, when we got to school, she punched Ben in the nose for ruining her romance story, her real-life romance with Warren from Warren AND HER WHOLE ENTIRE LIFE. It was a darned shame because

Gabby was away sick and she would have loved dealing with all that blood and bruising.

Worms spent the day carrying Feathers around inside his jumper in case he got cold. Everyone thought he was silly, but it turned out to be lucky. When the Colonel opened the door to the pigeon coop today, all the pigeons flew out and headed off towards Wagga Wagga. Only Feathers stayed behind because he was asleep, snuggled up against Worms's chest.

I was about to give a loud laugh, full of scorn and ridicule, but the Colonel looked devastated.

'Never mind,' I said encouragingly. 'They're sure to be back by sundown.'

And then, before I realised what I was doing, I *smiled* and gave him a *hug*.

WHAT WAS I THINKING????

I'm so confused!

Do I want to get rid of the Colonel or not?

Tuesday, 5 June

Seven carrier pigeons were sitting in the pigeon coop when we arrived at school. Everyone was so excited, except for Banjo, Mat and me. It was kind of obvious that they weren't the same pigeons as we had yesterday. Whitey had grown big brown spots, Blacky had turned dark grey overnight, Patch's patches had shrunk and Tiny Tim was now the smallest pigeon of them all.

I mentioned this to Mr Cluff. He said not to tell anyone, but the Colonel had driven all the way over to Gilgandra last night to pick up some new pigeons, just so the little kids wouldn't be sad. I was going to point out that he probably didn't want people to see that he'd messed up the whole pigeon thing YET AGAIN, but I didn't. It really was very kind of him, and the pigeons are beautiful. They're one of the best things we've ever had at school.

Lucy and Gabby spent all of lunch time shampooing Whitey to try to get the brown spots off his feathers. Jack and Davo spent all of recess and lunch time trying to feed their chocolate crackles and chips to Tiny Tim to fatten him up again. They also handed me another article for the newspaper:

Carrier pigeons — Part 2

Carrier pigeons are very sensitive animals. They need to be treated carefully because any small upset can have very bad consequences for their health.

For egg sample, if your pigeon gets stressed and worries a lot, its feathers can turn grey. Just like Davo's mum's hair is turning grey because Davo stresses her out all the time. Blacky worried so much when he was lost last night that he has already started turning grey.

Another egg sample is that too much exercise and not enough food can make your pigeon lose a lot of weight. If your carrier pigeon is going on a long journey, he should have a backpack filled with nutritious snacks like wheat, muesli bars and carrot sticks. Tiny Tim flew so far last night that he has lost at least fifty kilos and is now on a fatten-me-up diet of chocolate crackles and salt and vinegar chips.*

* Never feed your pigeons chicken chips. They are not cannibals.

Mrs Whittington wandered past the chicken coop this evening and Flipper went bonkers. He tumbled backwards into a corner, shook all over and hid his head beneath his wing. Poor thing.

Wednesday, 6 June

Woken at 6 am by the foxes. Wes and Fez climbed up onto the roof and pelted boots, rocks and scones down at them. Mum was really mad because the scones were to take for the Queen's Birthday morning tea at the CWA.

The Colonel gave us an advanced climbing course today. We revised wall walking, swinging and winching. Then the Colonel led us around to the end of the sports shed where he had set up a climbing wall by screwing hand and foot grips into the bricks. It was so cool. He said that we could use it any time we liked once we'd learnt to climb safely.

We spent the rest of the day rotating around five groups: walking up and down the toilet walls, swinging like Tarzan across Sam's compost heap, winching ourselves up the flagpole, scrambling on our tummies along the balance beam and traversing the sports shed wall. It was great fun. Even Matilda Jane the Mature loved it. She forgot to be angry with Ben and cheered when he made it across the new climbing wall.

Unfortunately, Sam fell into his compost heap when he was swinging across, and killed his favourite worm. He felt really bad. Gabby felt pretty crook too. She tried to revive the worm with mouth-to-mouth resuscitation, breathed in too hard and swallowed it.

Just as we were all walking out the front gate at home time, Dora called out from the top of the flagpole, 'Excuse me! I'd like to get down now!' Fair enough, too. She'd been stuck up there for nearly an hour.

Wes and Fez spent all evening screwing little blocks of wood to the wall outside their bedroom and rigging up ropes all over the veranda. Mum will freak when she sees all the holes they've drilled into the mud walls.

Normally I would point out every single bit of destruction to Mum then blame it on the Colonel but, honestly, it JUST DOESN'T WORK. Everyone loves him.

And why wouldn't they? He really is heaps of fun.

Besides, we all know that Wes and Fez are totally feral regardless of who is teaching them and what new ideas are put into their heads.

I give up. My plan to get rid of the Colonel has failed.

In fact, if I'm honest, I really don't want to get rid of him.

It's time to get Miss McKenzie back using Plan B …

Only trouble is, I don't have a Plan B!

Thursday, 7 June

Received three articles for the next paper today.

'Zombie flesh-eater let loose at primary school' by Sam tells of Gabby's unsuccessful attempt to resuscitate Anthony the worm.

'My life as a flag' has been written by Dora with a little help from her mum:

My life as a flag — A true story

I was flapping in the wind at the top of a pole. Nobody would look up.

Luckily I am a talking flag and I said, 'Excuse me. I'd like to get down now.'

Good manners are important, even when you are a flag.

They got me down and I lived happily ever after.

'Cake crumbs in the shape of Queen Elizabeth' by Mrs Flanagan tells of an amazing discovery at the CWA morning tea yesterday. When everyone had eaten a slice of Betty Simpson's ginger fluff sponge, the plate was covered in crumbs that looked *exactly* like Queen Elizabeth's head. Mrs Flanagan has included a photo and asked that I send a copy of the next *Bake*

85

Tribulation to the Queen herself! How exciting will that be?

Wes and Fez were late for dinner tonight. When Mum called them, they climbed through their bedroom window, traversed the wall outside using the blocks of wood they screwed in last night, winched themselves up to the roof, scrambled on their tummies along the top of the house, slid down the other side of the roof and abseiled down inside the old chimney into the dining room. It was amazing.

Mum was pretty mad. Not only were they late for dinner, but they'd knocked a dead magpie out of the chimney on the way down. Petal flapped up onto the dining table with fright and pooped on Dad's mashed potato.

Dad just scraped the mashed potato into the pig slops bucket and said, 'Oh, well ... I s'pose it could be worse.'

And he was right. Halfway through dinner the whole chimney caved in and made an awful mess of bricks, bird nests, soot and dirt. It took us until 9.30 to clean it all up.

This time tomorrow, Sophie, Peter and Peter's friend Xiu will be home from boarding school for the long weekend. I can't wait.

Friday, 8 June

Wes and Fez gave me their next manners column for the newspaper this morning:

Wes and Fez's modern manners

This week we look at being late for dinner. It is very rude to be late for dinner and your mum is sure to get really cross. She might even say you can't have dessert because you are a naughty, ungrateful child. But if you have some excuses ready, you won't seem rude and your mum won't tip your ice cream in the pig slops bucket.

These are our top six excuses for being late for dinner:

1. I was washing maggots off my hands.
2. I had my undies on back to front and had to put them on the right way.
3. I was reading the dictionary.
4. The pig wouldn't let my leg out of his teeth.
5. I was helping an old lady across the street.
6. I was doing my homework (only use this excuse if you are *really* desperate because your mum probably won't believe it).

We let the new carrier pigeons out of their coop today. They soared up into the air, around the school in a big loop and came back home again. What a relief!

The Colonel wriggled his hairy eyebrows up and down and said, 'Well boil the billy and pour the tea! Looks like we have the right pigeons at last!'

I smiled and gave him the thumbs up.

Sophie, Peter and Xiu met us at the Hillrose Poo sign with the pig chariots this afternoon. Peter, Wes and Doris raced Xiu, Fez and Mildred back to the house. Sophie and I drove the ute in front of them so they had to gallop through a cloud of dust. Giggled all the way.

It's so good to have them home from boarding school, even if it is just for the long weekend. Us Westons are all born with red dirt between our toes. We belong at Hillrose Poo.

This evening when Mum called us all in for dinner, Wes and Fez took Peter and Xiu the long way round. They climbed up the tank stand onto the guttering, scrambled along the top of the roof on their tummies, slid onto the veranda roof, swung down on a rope and dived through the dining-room window. They were all late for dinner.

Fez said, 'Sorry we're late, Mummy Darling Heart. Xiu had his undies on back to front and we had to wait until he put them around the right way.'

Good grief!

Saturday, 9 June

Wes, Fez, Peter and Xiu have spent the entire day making stuff in the machinery shed and digging ditches around the chicken coop (???). Xiu has brought a suitcase full of fireworks from his parents' pyrotechnics company in Kuala Lumpur, so things could get ugly before the weekend is through.

Mrs Sweeney, Mat and Lynette came over for the afternoon. Mum and Mrs Sweeney wanted to bake up a storm for the party tomorrow night — pavlovas, caramel meringue pies, apple turnovers and sausage rolls. We always have a huge bonfire with neighbours and friends to celebrate the Queen's Birthday.

Sophie, Mat, Lynette and I hid out in the tree house eating lamingtons. Sophie and Mat went feral talking about fashion and romance and LOVE. I thought it was going to be a total waste of time, until they started talking about

Miss McKenzie and Mr Cluff. Sophie said if we can't get Miss McKenzie to return to Hardbake Plains on her own, maybe we should convince Mr Cluff to go over to Scotland and bring her back.

It sounded like a great idea to me.

But then Mat started ferreting on and on about how romantic it would be and that they would probably be engaged on the wild, windy moors of Scotland and would then return to Australia to be married and Mat would be the chief bridesmaid and would wear a dress of rose pink satin and frangipanis in her hair and blah, blah, blah … spew, yuck, poo … blabber, blabber, blabber …

I grabbed Lynette and wandered over to Magpie's Rest to talk to Mrs Whittington and the pigs. Gertrude, Doris and Mildred are so much more intelligent than Matilda Jane the Mature.

Helped Mrs Whittington cut out red paper hearts for Valentine's Day. She gets a bit confused about celebrations but I don't suppose Queen Elizabeth would mind seeing love hearts everywhere on her birthday.

Monday, 11 June — 5 am!!!

Happy birthday, Queen Elizabeth.

Had the most amazing Queen's Birthday celebration ever. Dad, Peter and Xiu dragged dead trees from all over the place to make the mother of all bonfires. By the time everyone had arrived it was blazing like the sun.

The Sweeneys, the O'Donnells, the Simpsons, the Hartleys, Mr Cluff and the Colonel all came.

Gavin O'Donnell is still totally in love with Mat, even though she no longer likes him. He brought her a bunch of flowers and a box of chocolates and followed her around like a bad smell all night. Mat followed Xiu around like a bad smell all night, so it looked like a procession — Xiu, then Mat, then Gavin, then Gertrude, Doris and Mildred. Gertrude could smell the chocolates and wouldn't give up until she'd knocked Mat to the ground and scoffed the whole box. Mildred and Doris ate the flowers.

We had the funniest singalong with Dad playing the violin and Mr Sweeney and Mrs Hartley playing guitars. The Colonel knew all these hilarious Scout songs with words like:

Gong-dongle-diggery-dam
I like a sandwich with cheese and ham
I butter it twice and cut it up small
And sail it down the waterfall.

I'm glad I've made my peace with the Colonel. He really is incredibly kind and funny.

At midnight Dad played 'God Save the Queen' and Xiu put on a fireworks display. It was incredible — sparkly fountains in every colour of the rainbow, exploding balls that threw out more exploding balls, stars that turned into silver puffs of smoke, howling rockets that went so high they disappeared, and little parachuting men that shot way up in the air then floated down to earth. What was truly amazing was that Wes and Fez sat quietly with Mum and Dad and watched … and nothing went wrong.

Except for when Mrs Whittington came out on the veranda of Magpie's Rest with a slingshot, yelled, 'Shoot the blighters before they land!'

and started firing rocks at Xiu's little parachuting men. But that really wasn't Wes and Fez's fault.

The Queen's Birthday Disaster of Hillrose Poo, however, *was* Wes and Fez's fault — and Peter and Xiu's.

The guests had just left at 4 am when Peter whispered, 'Foxes approaching.'

Xiu hissed, 'Operation Boom,' and threw himself behind the lavender bush near the clothesline. Wes, Fez and Peter followed, so Sophie and I hid with them. We could just see the foxes creeping towards the chicken coop in the light of the bonfire.

Xiu struck a match and lit a piece of string that poked through the lavender bush. It hissed and sizzled, and began to sparkle its way across the yard towards the chicken coop.

Xiu leapt up and yelled something fierce in Chinese.

Gunther leapt off the veranda and ran towards the foxes, squealing and frothing at the mouth.

Fez leapt up and yelled, 'NOOOOOOOOO!!!!!'

Then there was an ALMIGHTY BANG. Rocks, splinters of timber, feathers, dust and dirt clouded the air.

The foxes could be heard yelping as they bolted away into the night. The chooks squawked and cackled hysterically. Flipper appeared through the dust, tumbling along the ground towards us at the speed of light. He bumped into Wes and sat there fluffing his feathers and quivering.

As the dust and smoke settled, we could see chooks running wildly around the yard. The chicken coop had a hole blown in the side. And Gunther lay on the ground, little bits of dirt and timber all over his lifeless body.

Fez ran towards him crying, 'No, no, no, no, nooooooooo!!!!'

Wes ran behind yelling, 'Gunther, darling Gunther!'

They threw themselves on him, sobbing uncontrollably and smothering him with kisses.

A hot, wet tear was just starting to dribble down my cheek, when Gunther groaned and opened his eyes. He squealed angrily, bit Fez on the ear, staggered to his feet, head-butted Wes and trotted off towards his bunnies. That pig is indestructible.

Well, almost. His tail had been blown off in the explosion and was left dangling on the chook yard fence, but other than that he seems fine.

Fez burst out crying again when he saw Gunther's tail.

Wes said not to worry because Gabby Woodhouse will be able to sew it back on using her first aid kit. They have stored the tail in the fridge in Mum's butter dish to keep it fresh.

What a night! I bet the Queen never has this much action at her own birthday party in Buckingham Palace.

8.20 pm

Convinced Fez that Gunther will have to live without his tail.

We buried it down behind the old pit dunny this afternoon, right next to Wendy the acrobatic sheep. Wes stuck a little cross on the grave that says:

RIP

Gunther's tail
May it curl with joy in Heaven
as it did on earth

Sophie and I said a prayer.

Peter and Xiu let off ten firecrackers, which I thought was in bad taste considering …

Fez said Gunther's tail was the most beautiful piece of pork he had ever seen, and burst into tears.

Tuesday, 12 June

Sophie, Peter and Xiu have returned to boarding school. It's not so bad though — they'll be back in less than four weeks for their mid-year break.

Gabby was really excited about Gunther's tooth marks in Fez's ear. She spent the whole bus trip this morning bandaging his head. He couldn't see a thing and walked straight into the flagpole when we arrived at school. Knocked himself clean out.

Mum had to come and take him to the doctor in Dubbo.

At lunch time, Mat painted my toenails (HUH?) then plucked my eyebrows. It was torture — both physically and emotionally — but it gave me a chance to talk to her about Sophie's idea for getting Miss McKenzie back.

Mat is so excited. She is going to wear a kilt to school each day and has promised to bring some of her mum's tartan ribbon for us both to tie in our hair. We will borrow Miss McKenzie's bagpipes from the school so that Nick can start playing 'My Bonnie Lies Over the Ocean' every recess and lunch time. And I will try to drop comments and random facts about Scotland into everyday conversation.

We're hoping that all this stuff will brainwash Mr Cluff so that he decides to travel to Scotland in the holidays. Then he can bring Miss McKenzie back home to Hardbake Plains.

Plan B, **MISSION McKENZIE**, just *has* to work.

Wednesday, 13 June

Mat wore a Scottish kilt to school today. We both wore tartan ribbons in our hair. I spoke with a Scottish accent all day long and had a very serious discussion with Mr Cluff about the Scots inventing golf.

MISSION McKENZIE was going fine until Nick started to play 'My Bonnie Lies Over the Ocean' on the bagpipes. The carrier pigeons went insane. They started thrashing around the coop, flinging themselves against the wire. The Colonel opened the door and they soared up into the air and flew off towards Broken Hill.

The Colonel said, 'Butter my crumpets! It's just like the Great Camel Stampede of Morocco in 1988. Had a whole herd of racing camels trained and ready to run the Desert Derby 2000 when the Viennese violinists started tuning up for their outdoor concert. Sounded worse than a flock of galahs singing opera. Camels didn't like it one bit. They gurgled, moaned and thrashed until they broke the fences. Charged off into the desert at the speed of light and never returned. Devastating loss of camel power. Put me off desert derbies for the rest of my life. Still, it wasn't all bad. Led me to walrus racing, and that really is a splendid sport ...'

He wriggled his bushy eyebrows and stared up at the sky.

Grace and Banjo burst out laughing. Ned nearly tripped over his own feet as he ran to tell Sam and Harry about the Colonel racing walruses.

The pigeons came back to roost by home time.

Thursday, 14 June

This morning, Mr Cluff and the Colonel announced that we are going on a bush safari in the state forest on Monday. Everyone is so excited.

The Colonel gave us a lesson on using compasses. He sorted us into six groups and gave each group a compass and a map of the schoolyard with north, south, east and west marked on it. There were six red X's that marked the spot of buried treasure.

Worms, Tom and I were the first to locate and dig up treasure. It was four little torches with clips to hang off our belts — how cool was that? Four other groups dug up tiny shovels, little water bottles, sewing kits and collapsible scissors.

The sixth group, Grace, Jack and Fez, got totally lost. Mr Cluff went looking for them when they hadn't turned up by recess. They were digging behind the pub — even though the map was of the schoolyard — and had found three chop bones, ten bottle tops and Barry Scott's false teeth.

Noticed Mr Cluff looking very thoughtful when he came across the map of Scotland that Mat and I had drawn in the dirt near Sam's vegie patch today. I'd even stuck a carrot in the exact location of Miss McKenzie's hometown, Dingwall. Hope **MISSION MCKENZIE** is working, despite the bagpipe disaster.

Friday, 15 June

Received FIVE more items for *The Bake Tribulation* today. Everyone is really getting into the spirit of having a local newspaper.

'Sunshine smiles' is an unbelievable news story by Mr Gillies. Sunshine is the grumpiest bloke this side of the Black Stump, but three different eyewitnesses swear that they saw him smile. It happened at the pub at 6.09 pm on Monday when Trevor McMahon tripped over the doormat and landed flat on his face.

'Nits and what you can do to avoid them' is an informative article written by Mr Cluff after eleven kids were sent home with lice today.

Tom handed in his next survey:

What is the most awful sound in the world?

❏ the bagpipes
❏ pigs squealing
❏ violins
❏ opera
❏ angle grinders cutting through steel
❏ fingernails scratching across a tabletop
❏ Hardbake Plains Carols by Candlelight
❏ your mum saying, 'Go and do your homework.'

Good choices, but it's going to be tough for people to decide.

Also got two more stories from Grace Simpson. One is about a pony and a fairy. The other is about three nits living on a fairy's head.

I'm going to Mat's for a sleepover tomorrow. It will be agony — all that nail polish and braiding and make-up and talk about LOVE. But I am being open to all experiences, even the really lame ones, and Mat really has been a great friend, helping out with **MISSION MCKENZIE** this week.

Saturday, 16 June

I am writing this while Mat and I sit and watch a movie called *You Make Me Smile*. So far it looks like it should be called *You Make Me Spew*. Everyone keeps sighing and giving each other these long, meaningful looks as though they have a bad case of indigestion.

We have spent *all day* doing our hair and make-up, trying on Mrs Sweeney's clothes (???) and talking about boys. I think we also did some exfoliating, but I can't be sure because I don't really know what exfoliating is!

Normally I would have been looking for a herd of stampeding hippos to throw myself under by lunch time, but we have also managed to come up with a fantastic new strategy for **MISSION MCKENZIE**. This month's edition of *The Bake Tribulation* is going to have a SCOTTISH THEME! How clever is that?

Every single page that Mr Cluff reads will remind him of Scotland and the radiant Katherine McKenzie so that he is driven *insane* with love and loneliness and simply *must* travel across the globe to be reunited with the *love of his life* (Mat's words, not mine!).

Mrs Sweeney has agreed to let us print her Scottish shortbread recipe. I am working on a Scottish comic strip.

Mat is going to change the next episode of *Heart's Triumph*. Elizabeth is going to be sent away to Scotland by her cruel father, and Edmund will be driven *insane* with love and loneliness and simply *must* travel across the globe to be reunited with the *love of his life* ... mushy, lovey, kissy, kissy ... blah, blah, blah ...

Whatever! As long as it works.

Sunday, 17 June

Mat and I sat up the back during Mass. Mat spent the whole service working on the Scottish episode of 'Heart's Triumph'. Gabby spent the whole service bandaging her little brother from head to toe. By the end of Mass he'd fallen asleep and looked like an Egyptian mummy.

Mrs Murphy ate three chocolate bars during the sermon. She would have eaten four, but Worms's tummy was rumbling so loudly she passed one to him.

This afternoon Mat and I baked three tins full of shortbread and practised drawing Scottish thistles.

MISSION McKENZIE is barrelling along!

Monday, 18 June

Had a fantastic day on our bush safari. Jack and Davo carried the pigeons in their own special little cage — except for Feathers. Worms carried Feathers stuffed down his jumper. The rest of us took water, food and ropes.

We started by making a big camp fire. The Colonel showed us how to get a flame by rubbing two sticks together. It was amazing. The rest of us tried, but all we managed to get was splinters and blisters.

Mr Cluff set up a whole heap of ropes activities across the gully. Mat was really getting into the

103

spirit of things until she tried to Tarzan swing across the creek. Her kilt got tangled in the rope, so she landed on the opposite bank dressed in her boots, cardigan and knickers. I don't know why she was so upset. They were very nice knickers — red with pink hearts all over. Even Grace Simpson commented on how pretty they looked.

The Colonel showed us a map of the state forest while we ate lunch by the fire. He placed the compass on top of the carrier pigeon cage for us all to see. Once we got our bearings, we headed out on the southern loop for a hike. At two o'clock we came out at Harry and Dora's farm in the complete opposite direction to where we should have been.

The Colonel stared at us with his bushy eyebrows wriggling up and down.

'Fiddlesticks and codswallop!' he cried.

He thinks the magnetite in the carrier pigeons' brains must have interfered with the magnet in the compass and given the wrong reading. It can happen. Some rocks and mountain ranges have magnetite in them too. They make it impossible to use a compass for direction.

Jack and Davo released the pigeons for their first flight home. We watched as they flew off towards their coop, then walked back in the same direction.

Back just in time to catch the bus at three o'clock.

Tuesday, 19 June

Received a poem from Banjo for *The Bake Tribulation* today.

A Lesson on Ropes

Swinging, swinging, swinging,
Like Tarzan in the trees.
Matilda in her tartan kilt
Feels a sudden breeze.
Her skirt is dangling from the rope.
Her knickers can be seen.
The moral of the story is:
For rope work, wear your jeans.

Mat *did* wear jeans today. However we are both still wearing tartan ribbons in our hair as a hint for Mr Cluff. **MISSION MCKENZIE** just *has* to work.

The Colonel took his class way out of town on their march this morning so they could let the carrier pigeons go. Once they've flown home a few times, we can start getting them to carry little messages.

All of the pigeons beat the junior class home, except for Feathers. He's so used to being carried around in Worms's jumper that he doesn't like to fly any more. Worms carried him back in his beanie.

Mat, Ben and I were sitting out in the sun reading our new play for English when the pigeons arrived home. Whitey and Patch landed on Mat's shoulders, fluffed up their chest feathers and cooed. Mat thought it was because they found her particularly attractive, but they just needed to do a poo. Mat walked around all day with two white trails down her back. I didn't tell her — I didn't want her to be embarrassed.

Wednesday, 20 June

Ben, Davo and Jack have been calling Mat 'Stripes' all day. She has no idea why, but it annoyed the guts out of her.

Tomorrow's *Bake Tribulation* should be perfect. Spent all morning with Ben putting the pieces of the newspaper together on the computer. I showed him again and again how to

PROOFREAD before he prints it out so there are no more disasters for poor Matilda Jane the Insane.

We have a record of *five* classifieds this edition, which is very exciting:

SAM'S VEGIES

All $2 each
bunch of radishes
5 beetroots
cauliflower
sack of potatoes
See Sam at the school vegie patch
(You can also pay with worms)

TOURISM SCOTLAND

There has never been a better time
to travel to Scotland and enjoy the wild
beauty of the Highlands.
Come and see Travel R Us — Dubbo

CHEAP SURGERY

Appendix need removing?

Aching bowels?

Leg needs replacing?

See Gabby

Early bird offer — tonsils removed for free

with every operation before 30 June

FOR SALE

Red woollen tartan kilt

Girl's size 14

$5 or nearest offer

Phone Matilda Jane

DINNER SPECIAL

<u>FREE</u> KNIFE AND FORK HIRE WITH
EVERY MEAL ON TUESDAY NIGHTS

Hardbake Plains Pub

Conditions apply:

• No loud talking

• Must buy three drinks with every meal

• Seating $2 extra

Ring Sunshine for bookings

MISSION McKENZIE is well on the way with the shortbread recipe, the Tourism Scotland ad, Mat's romance serial and this comic that I finished last night:

I have asked Ben to border each page of the newspaper with a Scottish design — thistles, bagpipes or tartan. I sure hope Mr Cluff gets the hint.

We took the carrier pigeons home with us on the school bus this afternoon. We let them go at Dora and Harry's front gate and Mr Cluff was going to lock them up when they flew back to school. Worms tried to set Feathers free but he kept flying back onto his shoulder and trying to hide down his jumper. Worms had to take him home for the night.

Thursday, 21 June

Did knot tying for today's outdoor adventure lesson. We learnt the overhand knot, the timber hitch, the noose, the half-hitch and exploding knots.

Ben said the half-hitch sounds like what you keep doing when your pants are too big.

The Colonel stared at Ben, his bushy eyebrows wriggling up and down and said, 'By golly gum it does too!' So he showed us a figure-eight knot that is perfect for holding your trousers up.

The rest of the knots were for climbing, putting up tents, building stretchers, trapping wild animals and tying up bundles of equipment.

Exploding knots are my favourite. They look like a real knot that can't be undone, but when you yank the ripcord (the end that hangs free) the knot explodes — that means it comes completely away from whatever it is tied to. How cool is that?

We each got a piece of fine rope to practise with, and I could do *everything*, including an exploding knot. Cassie learnt to tie her own shoelaces for the first time ever. Gary and Davo tied Banjo to the monkey bars upside down. Mat knotted her rope into a heart-shaped wall-hanging to display in our year seven study room. Very handy for surviving in the wilderness!

Wes was home sick with a tummy bug today. At least that's what Mum thinks it is, but I reckon it might be from all the cat food he ate last night when he and Fez played Truth or Dare. He was dead jealous when he heard that he'd missed out on exploding knots. He's asked Mum and Dad for some dynamite for his next birthday!

Friday, 22 June

Third edition of *The Bake Tribulation* came out today and it sure has been a tribulation. Ben did an all-time dodgy job of the printing. The classifieds were *totally* scrambled:

TOURISM SCOTLAND

There has never been a better time to travel to Scotland and enjoy the wild Highlands.
Come see Travel R Us — Dubbo
Early bird offer — tonsils removed for free with every tour before 30 June

---

GABBY NEEDS REPLACING

FOR SALE

Red aching bowels with worms
$5 or nearest offer
Phone Matilda Jane

SAM'S VEGIE SURGERY

Sack of potatoes need removing?
Size 14 radishes talking?
See Sam in his hip woollen
tartan kilt

DINNER SPECIAL

FREE BEETROOT, CAULIFLOWER AND
APPENDIX WITH EVERY MEAL ON
TUESDAY NIGHTS
Hardbake Plains Pub
Conditions apply:
• No loud girls
• Must buy three drinks with every meal
• Seating $2 extra
Ring Sunshine for bookings

Three different products for treating nits have been included in the ingredients list of Mrs Sweeney's Scottish shortbread recipe, and part three of 'Heart's Triumph' has to be seen to be believed:

Heart's Triumph — Part 3

Elizabeth was met at home by her angry father, Barry the butcher.

'How dare you swoon and sigh and kiss that man when you should be at home doing the housework, and making my dinner!' he growled. 'I'll teach you, young lady!'

Barry dragged Elizabeth down the street to the harbour.

Elizabeth cried, 'Edmund, oh Edmund, save me!'

But, alas, Edmund was nowhere to be seen.

Barry sold Elizabeth to a pirate from Scotland. She was forced to swab the deck, bake the shortbread and play the bagpipes all day and all night on the long voyage to Scotland. If she had a moment's rest, she would gaze out to sea and weep, 'Edmund, oh Edmund my love. Please find me. I am lost without you, oh Edmund my love.'

When Edmund heard what had happened to his beloved Elizabeth, he ran to the harbour, bought a ship, and set sail immediately for Scotland. But, alas, a great storm tossed the ship hither and thither and it was shipwrecked on a desert island. Edmund worked night and day, building a new ship from coconut shells and palm leaves. He was determined to find his beloved.

Finally, after six years, Edmund set sail and arrived in Scotland. He trekked across the highlands, battling Scottish longhorn cattle, wild haggises and blizzards. Finally he came to a small village and saw a tall, slender woman of overwhelming beauty. It was his beloved Elizabeth.

'Elizabeth!' he cried.

Elizabeth was overwhelmed at the sight of Edmund. She clutched her chest, fluttered her eyelashes and fanned her face. It was like a totally romantic moment.

'My one true love,' she cried. 'I knew you would find me. But what took you so long to come to me?'

Edmund clasped her to his chest and said, 'You will barely believe me, but I will tell you anyway.

1. I was washing maggots off my hands.
2. I had my undies on back to front and had to put them on the right way.
3. I was reading the dictionary.
4. The pig wouldn't let my leg out of his teeth.
5. I was helping an old lady across the street.
6. I was doing my homework.

Good grief! Stay tuned for the next episode of 'Heart's Triumph' to see if Elizabeth believes him!

Matilda Jane the Delicate Genius is going to FREAK when she reads this!

Saturday, 23 June

Phew! What a day!

Woken at 7 am by Fez screaming hysterically. Mildred had dug up Gunther's tail and was eating it.

Then Mat rang, sobbing her guts out. She said Ben had ruined her life ... AGAIN. There's *no way* Elizabeth could possibly love Edmund after all those ridiculous excuses for taking so long to find her. How on earth could she go on writing 'Heart's Triumph'?

Thankfully she doesn't seem to have noticed the ad where she is selling her aching bowels.

Mrs Whittington came over just before lunch, asking if we had any Nits Away Shampoo, Lice Be Gone Hair Gel or Nit Buster Powder. She was making Mrs Sweeney's Scottish Shortbread and didn't have three of the ingredients. Mum tried to convince her that she could make it just fine without the lice treatments, but she wouldn't listen. She got quite agitated and headed off across the paddocks with the pigs and Macka, in search of a chemist. Mum and I took two hours to get her home again.

We just got home when Sunshine rang. He was mad as could be. He said there was *no way* he was giving away free beetroot and cauliflower with meals at the pub on Tuesday night. He'd never make any money. And he didn't even know *how* to cook an appendix! He said some very rude words that grown-ups should never say to innocent children like myself, then hung up. Grumpy old bogan.

Then, at three o'clock, Charlene from Travel R Us rang to ask if I knew why they had a rush on Hardbake Plains customers with sore throats booking tours to Scotland. I lied. I'm not proud of it, but I did. I said it was probably just one of those weird coincidences that happen every now and then.

I never knew being chief editor would be so stressful. I thought I'd just accept everyone's articles and decide where they would go in the paper. I didn't dream that I would have half the community yelling at me.

I don't think I'll be sending *The Bake Tribulation* to the Queen. Maybe Mrs Flanagan can just send the photo of the cake crumbs instead.

At least Wes cheered me up at the end of the day. He was making exploding knots. He used three firecrackers to blow up each knot, and it really did give an amazing explosion every time.

I suppose Fez and I should tell him the real way to make exploding knots before he does any harm.

Sunday, 24 June

Wes blew the tail feathers off Flipper. He was tumbling past just as Wes let off one of his exploding knots.

Poor little pigeon. He's been nervous enough with Mrs Whittington using him as a hockey ball and Xiu blowing a hole in the side of the chicken coop. Now he's just a shivering blob.

I've had to take him inside with Petal and he waddles around with her wherever she goes. Petal looks a bit annoyed but I suppose she'll get used to it.

I told Wes the truth about exploding knots. I tied one around his wrist and pulled the ripcord, and it fell straight off.

117

He said, 'That's totally lame,' and walked away.

Mat rang tonight, hysterical. She'd reread the paper and noticed the ad.

'Everyone will think I have bowel problems,' she howled, 'And it says I have worms too! It's just like my horse Sheba and the gas problem all over again ...'

I tried to cheer her up by pointing out that at least she might make $5 out of it, but she just screeched in agony and hung up. At least it's taken her mind off Edmund and Elizabeth ...

Monday, 25 June

Took Flipper to school with Petal and me. He's still a terrified blob and can't be left alone. He sat in the corner of our year seven study room all day, fluffing his chest feathers up and shivering. The only time he looked happy was when Sarah fed him some nits from a little tin she took from her pocket.

Gabby Woodhouse is cross. She thinks the ad 'GABBY NEEDS REPLACING' was put in the paper by someone who wants to take her job as the school doctor. She offered to fix Mat's red aching bowels this morning and was highly suspicious when Mat screamed that she didn't even have a bowel problem. She thinks Mat is seeing someone else for first aid. It was a very emotional day.

It hasn't all been bad, though. Sam didn't mind the idea of wearing a woollen tartan kilt in his vegie patch, and I have had heaps of kids and adults tell me how much they love seeing each new episode of 'Heart's Triumph'. They think it's one of the funniest stories they've ever read.

Best of all, I saw Mr Cluff chewing thoughtfully on some shortbread as he flicked through *The Bake Tribulation* at lunch time. He even smiled once or twice. **MISSION McKENZIE** might just be working.

Tuesday, 26 June

Fantastic! Mr Cluff walked around the playground whistling 'Scotland the Brave' over and over again today. Before he knows it, he'll be totally brainwashed with thoughts of Scotland.

Had an important *Bake Tribulation* executive meeting with Ben and Mat this afternoon. Mat refuses to write any more of 'Heart's Triumph'. She said it is totally ruined. I told her that everybody thinks it's hilarious, but she just gave me one of those withering looks.

Ben said not to worry. He'd write 'Heart's Triumph' instead!

HELP!!!

Mat said she wants to use her wisdom and maturity to write something that will help others in the community. She wouldn't say what, but from the important look on her face, I know it's going to be something scary. It was bad enough in term one when she became the Love Mechanic and started giving everyone dodgy relationship advice. What will she try next?

This editor's job is getting VERY STRESSFUL.

Wednesday, 27 June

Flipper played with Feathers today. They sat on Worms's jumper, cooing and nibbling each other's beaks, while Worms, Banjo and I talked about our favourite desserts. I hope Flipper regains his confidence soon.

The Colonel has decided to prepare our minds as well as our bodies for camp. He says good soldiers need to use their brains first if they are going to get out of a sticky situation. Quick, creative thinking is the key to survival.

Of course, this means that Wes, Fez, Ben, Davo and Jack could be in real trouble. You can't use your brain first if you don't even have a brain!

The Colonel gathered us all into his classroom before home time today. He leaned forward, wriggled his hairy eyebrows and said, 'You are being chased across the African savannah by an angry rhinoceros!'

Everyone was dead silent. Cassie climbed onto my lap and started sucking her thumb.

The Colonel boomed, 'Suddenly, unexpectedly, you find yourself at the edge of a crocodile-infested river. The crocodiles are starving and alert, eager for a meal. The rhinoceros is furious, snorting steam from his nostrils, barrelling towards you at an alarming rate. You reach into your pocket but find only a mirror and a tube of lipstick. What will you do?'

Mat smoothed her hair behind her ears and said, 'What colour is the lipstick?'

Ben said, 'I'm not carrying lipstick in my pocket! How lame would that be?'

Dora Wilson burst into tears, sobbing, 'I'm too young to die. Why did you take me to such a dangerous place when I'm only five?'

Banjo said, 'Is there any word in English that rhymes with rhinoceros?'

Nick jumped up and yelled, 'I know! I'd smash the mirror and use the sharp edge to saw off the rhinoceros's horn so he couldn't hurt me.'

Mat said, 'Is the lipstick waterproof?'

I suppose she wants to be sure that it won't smudge when she jumps into the river to be mauled by crocodiles.

Thankfully the Colonel put us all out of our misery and said, 'I'd use the mirror to reflect sunlight directly into the rhinoceros's eyes to confuse it, then make my escape while it is wandering around in a daze.'

Sounded sensible enough until Gary asked, 'What if it's a cloudy day?'

The Colonel looked stunned for a moment, then said, 'Well pepper my legs! I didn't think of that! I suppose I'd have to shove the lipstick up his nose, leapfrog over his back and run for my jolly life!'

Everyone burst out laughing.

Except for Mat, that is. She thinks it is wasteful to go sticking lipstick up a rhinoceros's nose when there are poor children all over Africa who don't even own an eyeliner or a decent lip gloss.

What planet is that girl living on?

Thursday, 28 June

The senior kids have been learning about explorers for the last few weeks. Mr Cluff thought it would be a fun topic to research before camp. Maybe he thinks all those stories about explorers getting lost, starving and dying will make the kids more sensible in the bush. Good luck with that!

These are two of the articles I received today for *The Bake Tribulation*:

Blaxland, Wentworth and Lawson
by Grace Simpson

When Sydney got really big, the settlers needed more land for growing vegetables and grazing animals, but the Blue Mountains were in the way. Blaxland, Wentworth and

Lawson set out on an expedition in 1813 to find a way across the mountains to new land. They set off with four packhorses, five dogs, three convicts and a real person.

The horses' names were Bobby, Cheryl, Black Beauty and Melissa. They were playful horses who loved to run.

One day when they got to the top of the mountains, Bobby said to the other horses, 'I will race you to the bottom.'

The horses galloped down the mountain, dodging trees, jumping rocks and leaping over brooks. They all reached the bottom together at exactly the same time. They whinnied and shook their manes and said well done to each other.

Just then a fairy flew down from the trees and said, 'You are such kind and loving ponies. I have come to reward you all.'

She threw magic glitter onto the ground and a beautiful picnic appeared for them to eat. They had green grass, strawberry milk and chicken sandwiches and lived happily ever after.

Paul Edmund Strzelecki
by Wesley Weston

Mount Kosciuszko is the tallest mountain in Australia. It is 2228 metres high.

Paul Edmund Strzelecki was an explorer from Poland. He went up to the top of Mount Kosciuszko in 1840 and did the highest wee in Australia. His mum was really proud of him. His dad was too.

Also received an article by Matilda Jane the Mature called 'Waterproof lipstick — everything you need to know'.

We took the carrier pigeons home on the bus and let them go just before Hillrose Poo. Feathers went home with Worms again.

Friday, 29 June

Had so much fun today. The Colonel has bought these tiny little capsules that strap to the pigeons' legs for carrying messages. This morning half the kids wrote notes on little pieces of paper, popped them into the capsules, then carried the pigeons deep into the state forest where they let them go. The rest of us met the pigeons back at the coop and read the messages.

125

The notes said silly things like:

What's brown and sticky? A stick.
or
Wes was here.
or
Help! I am lost in the bush and Worms is looking at me like I'm a giant hamburger.

Nick sent a love letter to Lynette.

Banjo sent this poem to me for *The Bake Tribulation*:

Pigeons

Oh the pigeon is a wondRous biRd
Useful foR so much
Like sending little messages
To keep youR fRiends in touch.
It can be plucked and steamed oR fRied
OR made into a pie,
OR flown oveR an enemy
To poop on them fRom high.

After recess we swapped over so the rest of us got a chance to send messages back. Mat wrote an anonymous message to Mr Cluff that said, *Rescue Katherine from Scotland.*

I wrote a little return poem for Banjo:

Roses are red,
Violets are blue.
This pigeon is sent
From me to you.
You need not duck
As it hovers above.
This message is sent
With friendship and love.

Hee hee hee!

Feathers didn't fly home with any messages. Worms had to carry him back and hand-deliver his message to the Colonel. It said: *WENS LUNCH?*

The pigeons got taken home by some of the kids this afternoon. They can send messages back to school before they leave home on Monday morning. We missed out, but Wes and Fez borrowed a little message capsule anyway. Not quite sure why.

Saturday, 30 June

Wes and Fez are training Flipper to be a carrier pigeon. They attached the little capsule to his leg and spent the morning sending messages from one end of the hallway to the other as Flipper tumbled back and forth. They sent really stupid notes like:

To Wes
You stink.
Love Fez
and
To Fez
You have nits up your nose.
From Wes

They rolled around on the floor laughing as though they were the funniest, most intelligent words they have ever written.

Actually, they probably *are* the most intelligent words they have ever written …

Started tidying my room up ready for when Sophie comes home next week. Sophie and Peter get four weeks' holidays in the middle of the year. We only get two. The people who run the boarding school obviously realise that it's cruel to take children away from their families and try to make up for it by giving them more holidays than normal. It's so wrong!

July

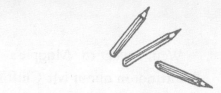

Sunday, 1 July

Mr Cluff called over today for a cuppa. He wanted to let Mum and Dad know that HE HAS BOOKED A TRIP TO SCOTLAND FOR THE SCHOOL HOLIDAYS.

MISSION McKENZIE is working!!!

Rang Mat and told her. She screamed so loudly that I dropped the phone. By the time I picked it up from the floor, she was planning a whole wedding and said that it was the Sweeneys' turn to have a wedding at their farm. She blabbered on and on about veils and flowers and satin and hosiery until I wanted to puke. I almost regret doing **MISSION McKENZIE**, but if it brings Miss McKenzie's beautiful, sparkly smile back into our lives it will be worth it.

I let Mat rant and rave a bit longer, then pretended that Dad needed me to help round up some sheep. Phew!

Went over to Magpie's Rest to tell Mrs Whittington about Mr Cluff's trip.

'That's lovely, dear,' she said. 'I miss Katherine terribly. Although not as much as I miss young Blue and her mother, Valmai. I haven't seen them since the end of World War II, you know.'

I gave her hand a squeeze. She stared at me as though she was trying to remember who I was.

As I left, she said, 'Thank you so much for praying with me, Father O'Malley. It's always a great comfort.'

Monday, 2 July

All of the carrier pigeons arrived back at school before recess today. Nick sent another love letter to Lynette. Cassie sent five sultanas for her morning tea. Jack sent his project on Australian explorers. The entire thing was written and illustrated on a tiny piece of paper the size of a five-dollar note.

Ben spent all morning reading a book called *Love's Journey*. The cover has a picture of a woman in a very short skirt fainting in the arms of a man dressed like Tarzan. They are in the jungle but she looks like she has just ironed her clothes, blow-dried her hair and put her make-up on. Looks exactly like something Matilda Jane or Sophie would read.

Ben said it was just for research before he writes the rest of Mat's romance serial, but he was really into it. By the time the bell rang for lunch, he was wiping his eyes with tissues, and I swear he sighed and whispered, 'How romantic.'

Scary, *scary* stuff!

Matilda Jane the Insane was creating her own romantic story all day long as she talked about **MISSION MCKENZIE**. I tried to point out that, so far, Mr Cluff was just *visiting* Miss McKenzie, but she gave me one of her withering stares and said I was clueless and totally immature.

Received an ad for the next paper from Sunshine today:

NOTHING IS FREE AT THE HARDBAKE PLAINS PUB.

No free beetroot.
No free cauliflower.
No free appendix.
No free cutlery hire.
No free use of toilets.
Get used to it or get lost.
Reminder Friendship Night 7–10 pm
Thursdays. Everyone welcome.

Tuesday, 3 July

Flipper finally got up the confidence to play outside today. He was frolicking around with Lucy's rabbits and Petal when he got all excited and tumbled off across the soccer pitch. Unfortunately he got caught up in the middle of the game just as Davo was dribbling the ball past. Davo kicked. Flipper flew up into the air and landed in the goal.

Davo ran around the field with his shirt pulled up over his head, yelling, 'Goal! Goal!'

Gary and Jack said there was no way it was a goal because the ball didn't go in. Davo and his team got really cross and said it was too. They started shoving and yelling, and there was a huge rumble.

Flipper sat in the corner of the soccer goal, puffing up his feathers and shivering. Gabby ran around and around the outside of the wrestling clump with her clipboard and first aid kit, looking for an injury to treat.

The Colonel stood by wriggling his eyebrows and said, 'Looks just like the Great Wrestling War of Wollongong back in 1991. Six hundred and fifty-four men wrestled for three days before it ended. All over an argument about whether sandwiches should be cut into squares or triangles. Triangles won, of course — and the world is a better place for it. Can't stand my lunch cut into squares. Barbaric habit.'

The Great Wrestling War of Hardbake Plains Soccer Field probably would have gone on for three days, too, if Mr Cluff hadn't rung the bell. By the time we went inside, Gabby had sent three boys and Flipper to the sick bay for bandaging.

Got an invitation to Matilda Jane the Mature's thirteenth birthday on Saturday. Sophie is invited too. It's a sleepover pamper party, whatever that means. Mat is beside herself with excitement. She has even given a list of suggested gifts, which I handed straight over to Mum. I have no idea what a loofah or an eyelash curler is.

Wednesday, 4 July

All the kids brought their sandwiches to school cut in triangles today.

Received three news reports for the paper about yesterday's fight. 'Liar! Liar! Pants on fire' by Gary and Jack gives quite the opposite

133

view of events to Davo's 'Jealous soccer team robs goal from brilliant player'. Gabby's report, 'Saved from the brink of death', tells the heroic story of how she treated Nick and Tom for grazed knees, Harry for dirty fingernails and Flipper for shock.

Ned handed in his survey results:

What is the most awful sound in the world?

Thank you to the fifty-nine people who replied. Every single person said that the Hardbake Plains Carols by Candlelight is the worst sound in the world by a long shot.

Also got this article about explorers from Fez:

Captain Cook

Captain Cook sailed on a ship called the *Endeavour.* He came from England in 1770 to sail in the Sydney to Hobart Yacht Race. He won because he was the only ship in it.

His crew all thought he was stupid and they were right. What is the point of a one-person yacht race? It's as dumb as a one-handed clap.

Mat spent the entire lunch break talking to Mr Cluff about Scotland and how great it will be for him to spend time with Katherine.

Katherine????

Since when did Miss McKenzie become *Katherine* for Matilda Jane the Insane?

Thursday, 5 July

Woken by the foxes at 4.20 am. We didn't think they'd come back again after the Queen's Birthday explosion.

Macka ran after them squealing and spitting, but Gunther ran away in the opposite direction. He bolted up the driveway towards the front gate, faster than a cheetah chasing a chicken. He didn't even wait for his bunnies to catch up. Poor thing. He must still be traumatised by losing his tail.

Wes and Fez spent the bus trip to school making slingshots out of forked sticks and rubber bands.

'It's for the foxes,' said Wes.

'To teach them a lesson,' said Fez.

'Yeah, and we don't just mean four times five is fifteen,' said Wes.

They broke three windows as soon as they arrived at school and hit Lynette right in the middle of her forehead with a rock. Gabby appeared from nowhere and bandaged Lynette's head, put her left arm in a sling and splinted both her legs. Nick appeared from nowhere and punched Wes in the guts and pushed Fez off the end of the veranda.

Mr Cluff confiscated the slingshots and gave Wes, Fez and Nick time-out. Wes and Fez used the time to write their next manners article for the newspaper.

Wes and Fez's modern manners

This week we look at saying sorry.

Sometimes, no matter how hard we try to be good little Vegemites, we do the wrong thing — like accidentally hitting someone with a plank of wood, accidentally calling someone a STINKY POO BUM or accidentally throwing a brick through the stained-glass window at church.

When you do the wrong thing you need to say sorry. It's good manners. Besides, if you don't, your mum will call you an ungrateful little rat or something worse.

You can say sorry with words

e.g. I'm sorry I called you a fat, ugly toad. It just slipped out.

I'm sorry I ran over your pet mouse with my bicycle. I'll never do it again.

You can say sorry by writing a letter

This is a good idea when you are too scared to be near the person to say sorry with words.

e.g. Dear Mummy Darling Heart

You are the best mummy in the world. You make the best mashed potato ever. You are pretty and kind and very understanding too.

Lots of love and hugs and kisses from your darling son.

P.S. I'm sorry I broke the spout off your antique teapot when I was drinking green cordial from it in the tree house.

Heard Wes and Fez apologising to Lynette at recess.

'I'm really sorry I hit you in the forehead with a rock,' said Wes.

'Yeah, he was aiming for your nose,' said Fez.

Friday, 6 July

Had a great end-of-term camp fire today. We made damper, which we wrapped around a stick and held over the fire to cook. Worms was starving. He held his damper right in the flame so it would cook faster. It caught on fire and turned into a hard black lump of charcoal. Worms was so upset that the Colonel had to feed him a packet of chocolate biscuits from the staffroom to calm him down.

We had another treasure hunt using maps and compasses. The Colonel said practice makes perfect. No-one ended up at the pub this time, but Tom, Sam and Dora did dig up the remains of Lucy's rabbit, Bella, who died last year. Grace, Gary, Harry and I found the real treasure — a bag of lollipops, which we shared around with everyone. Except for Matilda Jane the Mature. She says sugar is bad for her complexion.

The juniors gave a marching demonstration before home time. They marched backwards, forwards and side to side. It looked more like line dancing than marching, but they were very proud of themselves anyway.

Mr Cluff finished the day with an end-of-term speech, wishing us all a safe and happy holiday. He said he would pass our love on to the gorgeous Miss McKenzie. He was blushing like a beetroot and grinning so much I thought his face was going to split. Mat and Ben looked at each other and said, 'How romantic!' at exactly the same time!

Sophie, Peter and Mum didn't get home from Bathurst until really late. Peter had been in trouble for putting a rat from the science lab inside one of the beanbags in the library. The librarian had fainted when it chewed a hole through the side and popped its head out to say hello.

Wes and Fez thought it sounded hilarious.

'I love rats,' said Fez.

'Yeah. Especially Super Rat,' said Wes.

'I miss Super Rat,' said Fez, and burst out crying.

Sunday, 8 July

Phew. Home at last. What a relief!

Sophie and I have been at Mat's sleepover pamper party with Lynette, Grace and Julia. Julia is Ben and Grace's big sister, who goes to boarding school. She's fifteen, like Sophie.

The idea of the party was to get into our pyjamas and watch romantic movies while we had beauty treatments. I felt like such a doofus. Everyone laughed when I came out in my blue-checked boys' flannelette pyjamas. They all had satin pyjamas with pink hearts and kittens all over them. Grace and Julia had satin bathrobes as well.

Mat *screamed* every time she opened a present. I don't know what Sophie and I gave her, but it came in five different little bottles and made her so happy that she fanned her face and rolled her eyes. Lucky Mum chose the present and not me. I was going to get her a plastic poncho and some waterproof matches to take on camp.

We covered our faces in green mud, smeared our feet with olive oil and wrapped them in cling wrap, and spread our hair with something that looked like raw eggs. I don't know why everyone was so concerned about my pyjamas, because we *all* looked like something from *Frankenstein* by the time we were done.

While our beauty treatments were soaking in, we watched a movie called *Forever and More* THREE TIMES. Mat cried *every* time, even when she *knew* that the boyfriend was going to go away to Iceland.

When we finally washed the face masks off, everyone's skin had turned green! It was hilarious.

I laughed and laughed until my tummy ached, but Mat, Sophie and Julia nearly died. Mat scrubbed her face with a nailbrush and took the skin off her chin, so now she has green skin *and* a big scab.

Mrs Sweeney still made us all go to Mass this morning. She said we couldn't possibly miss it when Father O'Malley only comes once a month. I didn't care. And I don't know why Sophie was so upset. She dyed her hair fairy-floss pink with food colouring once. That looked heaps worse than the green skin.

Mat wore sunglasses and a scarf around her head to Mass, but you could still see her scabby chin and green skin. She burst out crying when Ben and Peter made frog noises. Julia hit Ben over the head with a prayer book.

It's a relief to be home now. Although if Sophie looks in the mirror and sobs one more time I might have to kill her …

Monday, 9 July

My face is still green as grass. Petal is quite excited by it. She keeps nibbling my cheeks.

Wes and Fez are dead jealous of Sophie and me. They want to be green too. They tried smearing green dishwashing liquid all over their faces, but it just got in their eyes and made them cry.

Peter gave me a news report for *The Bake Tribulation* today. 'Alien invasion' tells of the terrifying experience church-goers had yesterday when Mass was invaded by six green-skinned Martians. Mat will be furious when she reads it.

I've written 'Skin deep', quite a serious article asking just how beautiful can a girl be if she doesn't have a brain. Really, there is nothing attractive about knowing that someone has a big, fat empty space between their ears, is there? Just ask Warren from Warren.

I also have three ads for the classifieds:

WANTED

Volunteers for medical experiments and practice operations.
See Gabby

PONY FOR SALE

Ideal for church picnics and barbecues.
Phone Doris

Sophie and I spent the afternoon over at Mrs
Whittington's cottage. She was sorting out her
pantry cupboard and wanted to store everything
in order of importance. She was quite upset when
she got to the baked beans and chicken noodle
soup, because she couldn't decide which had to
go first. Sophie thought the soup was the most
important. Mrs W thought maybe the baked
beans were. I suggested we just eat them both so
we didn't have to decide. So we had baked beans,
chicken noodle soup, orange cake and hot
chocolate for afternoon tea. Problem solved!

Tuesday, 10 July

Foxes at 5.15 am. Wes, Fez and Peter ran out
with slingshots to attack. Fez lost control and his
slingshot fired back into Wes's face. He tried to
kiss Wes to make it better but Wes shoved him

143

away and called him a sissy pink-pants. Fez shoved Wes, Wes punched Fez, and a big rumble started. Peter had to shoot them three times with his slingshot before they'd break it up. The foxes ran wild and free as usual.

Sophie and I are still green.

So are Wes and Fez. They coloured their faces in with green permanent markers today. Mum freaked. She was going to take us all in to Dubbo for a family photo on Friday. Guess she'll have to save it for some other time.

Wednesday, 11 July

Overheard Mum talking to Dad late last night. She said things like, 'They have to go,' and, 'Get rid of them once and for all before they do any harm.'

I really hope she was talking about Wes and Fez, but suspect she was talking about the foxes.

Mr Cluff has emailed a Scottish article for *The Bake Tribulation*, just like he promised. 'Australian teacher almost attacked by Loch Ness monster' is a sensational headline. The story, however, is dead boring. The loch where he was swimming turned out to be a dam, and the monster turned out to be an old gumboot floating in the water.

I suppose Mr Cluff has better things to do than go on wild adventures. Hopefully he is spending most of his time talking Miss McKenzie into coming back to Hardbake Plains. It shouldn't be too difficult if the most exciting thing happening at Dingwall is the discovery of a gumboot in the dam.

I think Peter's 'Alien invasion' will have to be the newspaper's lead story this time. Either that or Gabby's article, 'Is wearing your undies back to front bad for your health?'

Thursday, 12 July

Mat's face is still green, just like mine. Saw her today at Ben's house when we met to finish organising *The Bake Tribulation*. Bucket, the postman, said he'll pick the newspapers up at Ben's farm tomorrow morning and deliver them around the community on his mail run.

Ben wouldn't show me part four of 'Heart's Triumph'. He said he wants it to be a surprise when I read the paper tomorrow. I'm sure it will be!

I was hoping that Mat's article, 'Waterproof lipstick — everything you need to know', might have been her idea of using her wisdom and maturity to help others in the community. No such luck.

She has written a questionnaire that will fill a whole page of *The Bake Tribulation*:

How mature are you?

It is important to know how mature you are. It is totally lame when you see immature people out and about trying to lead normal, happy lives. Take this quick quiz to find out the truth about yourself:

1. *What do you do when you look through fashion magazines?*
   a) *Decide which clothes and make-up you would look good in.*
   b) *Point to the clothes you hate and say, 'Yuck!'*
   c) *Draw moustaches and vampire teeth on all the models.*

2. *What do you do when someone tells a funny joke?*
   a) *Smile carefully so that you don't scrunch your face up too much.*
   b) *Laugh and smile with your mouth open.*
   c) *Laugh so hard that you snort like a pig.*

3. What do you do when a boy burps out loud?
   a) Give him a withering stare.
   b) Say, 'That's gross,' but laugh a bit anyway.
   c) See if you can do an even bigger burp just to show off.

4. If you are walking along and see a dog poo on the ground, what do you do?
   a) Roll your eyes and fan your face until someone removes it.
   b) Screw up your face and say, 'Poo!'
   c) Kick it out of the way and laugh so hard that you snort like a pig.

5. What is your favourite thing to do on a quiet evening at home?
   a) File your fingernails and watch a romantic movie.
   b) Play Monopoly and eat chocolate biscuits.
   c) Run around in the dark playing spotlight and hunting rats.

6. *A handsome boy asks you out on a date. What do you do?*
   a) *Flutter your eyelashes and say, 'Thank you. That would be delightful.'*
   b) *Say, 'I'll have to check with my mum first.'*
   c) *Laugh so hard that you snort like a pig.*

7. *An ugly boy asks you on a date. What do you do?*
   a) *Give him a withering stare and say, 'I don't think so!'*
   b) *Say, 'I'll have to check with my mum first.'*
   c) *Accept and go on a date so that you don't hurt his feelings.*

Scoring: Score 10 points for every a, 5 points for every b, 1 point for every c.

What your total score means:
7–15 You are completely immature. I don't mean to sound cruel, but you are a total embarrassment to your family and friends. There is no hope for you.
16–45 You are quite immature but there is hope. Grow up and stop acting like a child.
46–70 Congratulations. You are mature, attractive and intelligent.

I am *totally* immature. I did the quiz when I got home and scored 7. What's wrong with laughing so hard that you snort like a pig? Or drawing moustaches and vampire teeth on the models in a magazine? That's not immature. It's just fun.

Friday, 13 July

Bucket delivered the mail and the fourth edition of *The Bake Tribulation* just before lunch. Everyone was arguing over who got to read it first, so Sophie read 'Heart's Triumph' out loud while we ate our sandwiches. It was unbelievable …

Heart's Triumph — Part 4

'Stone the crows!' cried Elizabeth. 'You have had a busy time. But now you are here with me — forever — with your undies on the right way.'

Edmund was just about to hug Elizabeth again when a wild haggis leapt out from the bushes, flung itself at Edmund and ripped his arm off.

'Edmund!' screeched Elizabeth, and she fainted, tripping back into Loch Ness as she fell.

The Loch Ness monster was starving. It swam through the water, thrashing with joy as it headed towards its first meal in months — Elizabeth burger.

'This'll be fully sick!' yelled the Loch Ness monster.

Edmund saw the monster getting closer and closer to Elizabeth. He kicked the wild haggis back into the bushes, picked up his torn-off arm, leapt into the water and beat the Loch Ness monster over the head with it. The monster grabbed Edmund's arm and chewed it up. Before he could swallow and start munching on Elizabeth, Edmund dragged her out of the lake to safety.

They collapsed on the shore, gasping for breath. Edmund gazed lovingly into Elizabeth's eyes that were like blue poo. Elizabeth gazed lovingly at Edmund's eyes which were like brown poo.

They were just about to kiss when a ferocious wolf, attracted by the smell of blood spurting from Edmund's shoulder where his arm had been ripped out, ran down from the highlands. It leapt from a rock and flew through the air towards Edmund, baring its fangs.

'Edmund!' screamed Elizabeth, her eyes popping out of her head.

The wolf leapt on Edmund, tore his leg off and ran away to the highlands again. Blood spurted everywhere, including all over the front of Elizabeth's beautiful satin gown.

'Oh Edmund,' she screamed. 'What are we going to do now?'

Peter was rolling around laughing his guts out. Sophie pushed her red jelly aside and couldn't bear to eat it. Wes and Fez ran into the lounge room to look up haggises on the internet. They reckon they sound amazing and want to get one for a pet.

I looked at the rest of *The Bake Tribulation* while I ate Sophie's jelly. I was relieved to find that Ben had been very careful with the printing this time. There was just a small double up with some of the print in Gabby's article and Sunshine's pub announcement. Sunshine's ad now says:

NOTHING IS FREE AT THE HARDBAKE PLAINS PUB.

No free beetroot.
No free cauliflower.
No free appendix.
No free cutlery hire.
No free use of toilets.
Get used to it or get lost.
Reminder — Friendship Night 7–10 pm Thursdays. Everyone WEARING YOUR UNDIES BACK TO FRONT welcome.

Saturday, 14 July

Went to the Town Hall this afternoon. Mum was meeting with the CWA ladies to judge the Amazing Cake Crumb Pictures competition. Heaps of other kids were there with their mums too.

Everyone was talking about Mat's questionnaire in *The Bake Tribulation*. Most kids said they turned out to be either quite immature or totally immature, except for Matilda Jane, of course.

Worms and Lucy weren't sure how they would act if a boy asked them out on a date. Lucy said it would depend on whether or not the boy liked rabbits. Worms said it would depend on whether or not the date was to a restaurant with one of those buffets where you could eat as much as you like.

Mat rolled her eyes at Worms and said the questionnaire was only meant for *girls*. Ben, Nick and Tom said *they* had all done it and turned out to be mature, attractive and intelligent.

Mat said that anyone who wrote a romance serial like part four of 'Heart's Triumph' could not possibly be mature, attractive or intelligent. It was a complete and utter disaster written by a total maniac.

Ben said he'd have to be more mature, attractive and intelligent than anyone with a green face and a scab the size of Tasmania on their chin. He *does* have a point there.

Mat burst out crying and ran outside. I found her under the tank stand half an hour later, eating a whole jam sponge roll. When she'd finished, the crumbs stuck to the plate were exactly the same shape as the scab on her chin. Amazing!

Sunday, 15 July

The foxes haven't returned.

Wes and Fez are still here.

Which makes me think that Mum actually meant the *foxes* when she said we had to get rid of them once and for all. Darn it! I hate these constant disappointments.

Sophie and I have faded to a pale shade of green. A couple of days and we should be back to normal. Wes and Fez might take a bit longer. They don't call them permanent markers for nothing.

Wes and Fez spent the afternoon drawing moustaches, glasses and vampire teeth on all the models in Sophie's fashion magazines. She freaked and said they were totally immature. Wes and Fez ran outside laughing so hard that they snorted like pigs.

Wrapped up a copy of *The Bake Tribulation* to post to Miss McKenzie tomorrow. I'm hoping it will be the last one I have to send. Maybe she will be able to read the next edition right here in Hardbake Plains!

Monday, 16 July

Mum took Sophie and me in to Dubbo today to go birthday shopping for Dad and Peter. Peter turns seventeen tomorrow. Dad's birthday is on the twenty-first.

We bought Peter a hat that has a real crocodile-skin band around it, a big jar of chocolate-coated peanuts and a red doona cover for his bed at boarding school. We bought Dad a new bow for his violin and a pair of blue flannelette pyjamas exactly the same as mine. Mum also got me a box of chocolates to use for a birthday treasure hunt.

Peter found a dead rat for Wes and Fez while we were out today. It's a bit squashed from being under a hay bale, but Wes and Fez are ecstatic. They've drawn glasses and a moustache on its face and called it Smart Rat.

'You can tell he's smart because of his glasses,' said Wes.

'And the wise look on his face,' said Fez.

'He's not as brave as Super Rat,' said Wes.

'But he's heaps smarter,' said Fez.

Yeah, right.

Tuesday, 17 July — Happy birthday, Peter!

Started the day with pancakes and presents for Peter. Wes and Fez had eaten all the chocolate-coated peanuts and filled the jar back up with rabbit poo. Now *there's* something totally immature Matilda Jane didn't mention in her questionnaire.

Sophie and I made the best birthday cake ever — a big, brown yabby. Then I fixed up a treasure hunt. Found two dead foxes hanging up on the fence while I was burying the treasure down at the shearing shed. Dad's hung them there as a warning to the other foxes to stay away.

Maybe we should dangle Wes and Fez upside down from the clothesline to warn other naughty boys to stay away. It may not work, but it sure would feel good to give it a try …

Peter and Dad came in from the machinery shed when Mum got home from her CWA meeting. We ate cake and did the buried treasure hunt. Dad followed the map as far as the hayshed and fell asleep on the top of the hay bales. Mrs Whittington walked all the way to the front gate with her shovel and dug out the Hillrose Poo sign.

Sophie and Peter are living proof that you learn nothing at boarding school. They thought they'd get to the treasure first by driving the old ute, and ended up at the back of the Hartleys' farm before they realised they'd taken a wrong turn somewhere.

Believe it or not, Wes, Fez and Smart Rat were the winners. They used their map and compass perfectly until they got to the spot where I had buried the treasure. They couldn't be bothered digging, so they used some of Xiu's leftover firecrackers to blow a hole in the dirt. The box of chocolates was totally blown to bits.

Wes and Fez came home covered in little shreds of coloured foil, chocolate flakes and splatters of caramel, strawberry cream and nougat. Gertrude, Mildred and Doris appeared from nowhere, barrelled them over and licked every last speck of chocolate from their faces and clothes.

Mildred chewed Smart Rat's front leg off. It had been covered in orange cream filling. It was just like Edmund and the wild haggis all over again.

Wednesday, 18 July

Smart Rat doesn't seem too troubled by his missing leg. He spent all day sitting on the lounge studying the dictionary.

Bucket delivered an article from Betty Simpson for the next *Bake Tribulation* today. 'Crumbs alive' reports on the CWA's Amazing Cake Crumb competition. It was a very strong field with photos of crumbs in the shape of many different things, including Germany, New South Wales, Father O'Malley's ear, the Opera House and three men panning for gold. But Mrs Love's marble cake crumbs in the shape of a five-legged sheep was the clear winner. It was such a success that the CWA have decided to run an Amazing Vegetables in the Shape of Famous People competition in November when we have the Garden and Flower Show.

Got hungry this afternoon and started nibbling on Peter's chocolate-coated peanuts. Yuck! I hate it when I forget to be on guard against Wes and Fez's stupidity.

Thursday, 19 July

Had a great time at the pub this evening. Heaps of people turned up for the Friendship Night wearing their undies back to front. A few people, including Peter, Wes and Fez, wore their undies over the top of their clothes, just so everyone could be sure that they had them on back to front. Dad, Mr Hartley and Mr Sweeney wore their undies on their heads.

Sunshine was as grumpy as a bear with a burr in its bum. He said we were lowering the tone of the pub.

Gabby was most upset about the risk to everyone's health. She ran around yelling, 'Didn't anyone read my article?'

Mat was in a foul mood. Not only was she surrounded by a whole community of totally immature people, she was still furious about Ben turning 'Heart's Triumph' into a horror story. She said he had ruined everything by putting in all that violence and robbing Edmund of his arm so that he can't hug Elizabeth properly.

Ben smirked and said, 'Edmund's all right — 'e's 'armless.'

I laughed so hard that I snorted like a pig. I really couldn't help it.

Mat wasn't amused.

Friday, 20 July

Received an ad from Sunshine for the paper today:

Flipper has made a new friend. Smart Rat sat under the tree house all afternoon reading *An Encyclopaedia of Dinosaurs* while Wes, Fez, Sophie and I made a camp fire. Flipper snuggled up to Smart Rat and cooed happily. It's the first time he's been out and about since the soccer match.

Petal is really jealous. She's spent weeks ignoring Flipper, but now he has a new friend she wants him back. She kept waddling back and forth, wagging her tail feathers angrily at Smart Rat. She pecked the corner off the page on stegosauruses.

We sat around the fire all evening, toasting marshmallows and singing the silly songs the Colonel had taught us. I made up my own song just for fun:

Gong-dongle-diggery-dat

I like a sandwich with chopped-up rat.

I fill it with whiskers and tails and toes

And use it at once to blow my nose.

Wes and Fez were really angry. Fez covered Smart Rat's ears and Wes glared at me.

'You're mean, Blue,' said Wes.

'And gross,' said Fez.

'You need to think before you act,' said Wes.

'And stop being so immature,' said Fez.

They stormed off inside with Smart Rat. Flipper tumbled after them, trying to keep up. Petal waddled after Flipper.

Sophie and I burst out laughing. I laughed so hard I snorted a bit of melted marshmallow out my nose. Gerty snuffled it up and ate it.

Gross!!

Saturday, 21 July — Happy birthday, Dad!!

Sophie and I spent all day making a farm birthday cake for Dad. We made a big, flat chocolate cake and covered it with grass, sheds, a tractor and sheep. The sheds were made of biscuits, the tractor was from our Lego and the sheep were made from marshmallows and toothpicks.

I accidentally splashed Sophie with the green food colouring when we were dyeing the coconut for the grass. Her face ended up covered in green freckles. They won't come off.

Wes and Fez were dead jealous. They said Sophie looked even cooler than when she was green all over, and started drawing coloured freckles on their own faces with felt-tip pens. Sophie thought they were making fun of her and got really cross. She grabbed Smart Rat by the neck and flushed him down the toilet.

The toilet clogged and overflowed, bringing up a whole heap of soggy toilet paper. While we were running around mopping up the mess, Petal flew up onto the kitchen bench and ate all the grass off the farm cake.

When Mum, Peter and Dad came in for the birthday afternoon tea, the house was covered in wet towels, dead marshmallow sheep, chocolate cake crumbs and a pongy smell that no-one should have to experience on their birthday. Sophie was leaning over the kitchen sink scrubbing her face with the dishcloth, bawling her eyes out. Fez was pushing clumps of toilet paper back down the loo with Dad's new violin bow and Wes was giving Smart Rat mouth-to-mouth resuscitation on the dining table. Flipper was standing nearby, shivering with suspense over whether Smart Rat would make it.

Mum freaked.

Dad just shrugged and said, 'Oh, well … I s'pose it could be worse.'

And he was right. Peter slipped on the wet floor and bashed his head on the corner of the dining table. Fez tore up Dad's new blue flannelette pyjamas to bandage his head.

Happy birthday, Dad!

Sunday, 22 July — Happy birthday, Dad (attempt two)!

Sophie, Mum and I made a big cream sponge for Dad today. We all sat down for afternoon tea, lit the candles and sang 'Happy Birthday to You'. Dad said there were so many candles that he needed our help. Wes leaned over, took a deep breath and sneezed all over the cake.

Mum rolled her eyes, took the cake out for the pigs and opened a packet of chocolate biscuits.

Wes, Fez and Smart Rat spent all evening writing their next manners column for *The Bake Tribulation*.

Wes and Fez's modern manners

This week we look at rude noises at the dinner table. It is not polite to sneeze, burp or break wind at the dinner table, but sometimes you just can't help it. It is important to know how to cover up these rude noises when you just can't hold them back.

Covering up a sneeze
Include the sneeze in a sentence so people don't know that it has even happened.

> e.g. ACHOO I saw at the sheep sales last week?
> ACHOO and chew but I can't seem to get through this steak.
> ACHOO-choo train goes toot-toot.

Covering up a burp
Including a burp in a sentence is not so easy. You can sing 'Happy Birthday' and include the burp in that — *Happy BURPday to you, happy birthday to you*. If it is not anyone's

birthday, then you just have to pretend that you got the date mixed up. It is rude to burp, but it is not rude to be stupid.

Covering up wind
It is easy to break wind without people thinking you are rude. You just need to look shocked and blame the noise on the dog, the squeaky chair or your brother.

Monday, 23 July

Back to school for Wes, Fez, Petal, Flipper, Smart Rat and me. Sophie and Peter are home for two more weeks — HOORAY!!

Mr Cluff is back from Scotland and full of joy. He just about *skipped* around the playground all day long. He wore a really daggy Scottish hat called a Tam o' Shanter — red tartan with a black pompom on top. Mat and I agree that **MISSION MCKENZIE** must have gone well, but we are both a bit concerned that Mr Cluff hasn't mentioned anything about Miss McKenzie coming home to Hardbake Plains.

The Colonel started the day with a very serious Soldiers-Prepare-for-Action speech. There is only one week to go! He encouraged us to start packing our backpacks and to practise our adventure and survival skills as much as we can over the next week leading up to camp.

We spent our recess and lunch time climbing, swinging on ropes and doing archery. Mat practised filing her fingernails and applying nail polish while sitting on a rock.

Worms practised going without food for as long as he could. He lasted for four minutes and twenty-seven seconds at recess before he ate three muesli bars, a banana muffin and a pear. At lunch time he only lasted for two minutes and fifty seconds, but he said that was because he had eaten such a small morning tea!

The Colonel took the carrier pigeons all the way to Dubbo after school this afternoon. He wanted to do a longer home run before we take them on camp. Hope they all turn up tomorrow.

Tuesday, 24 July

The carrier pigeons were all back at school. Each of them delivered a little message to prepare us for camp, like:

A good soldier always carries a clean handkerchief
A tidy camper is a happy camper
Be prepared for anything

Ned is really keen to be prepared. At recess he filled his backpack with his sandwiches, a handkerchief, Gabby's thermometer and bandages, Blacky the carrier pigeon, a game of Scrabble and his pencil case. He climbed right up to the top of the big gumtree to practise his climbing skills and couldn't get down again.

Nobody even noticed he was stuck until Scrabble letters and tears started falling from the sky. I think he was trying to spell out a sentence like, 'Will someone please rescue me?' but the letters didn't fall in the right order. Nick got cross because he found a group of letters at Lynette's feet that said SCUM.

Mr Cluff was about to ring the Bush Fire Brigade, but the Colonel said, 'Don't worry! I know exactly what to do. The Fifth Regiment of the Pink Paratroopers was faced with the same dilemma in 1977. Their sergeant was caught in the top branches of a kauri tree when parachuting into New Zealand during the Great Kiwi Rebellion of 1977.'

He wriggled his hairy eyebrows and disappeared inside. When he came back he had ropes, two helmets, a block of chocolate and a harness. He climbed up the tree, gave the chocolate to Ned as a distraction, harnessed him up, and lowered him down from the treetop.

Ned had just landed on the ground when Nick ran over and kicked him in the shins for insulting Lynette. Gabby, was beside herself with joy that there was at least one injury to treat. She took Ned to the sick bay and bandaged his head.

Wednesday, 25 July

Received Gabby's latest first aid article for *The Bake Tribulation*, 'To bandage or not to bandage'. It's quite surprising how often a bandage should be used. There are the obvious cases, like for a sprained ankle, a badly grazed knee or a gash to the forehead. But I think our readers will be surprised to know how important it is to bandage in cases of toothache, constipation, hiccups, broken fingernails and warts. I think they will also be surprised to know where some of the bandages should go.

Mat has been quite stressed about packing for camp. We are only allowed a small overnight bag and a backpack. We already have a list of what to bring in our overnight bags, so our pack is the only space we have for personal items.

I still have loads of room after putting in a drink bottle, tissues, sticking plaster, a block of chocolate, waterproof matches, a little torch, my diary and a pen. Mat asked if she could use some of my space, but I said no. The whole idea is that we take responsibility for our own things on camp. Besides, what could Mat possibly need that would fill her backpack *and* mine? It's just for one night.

Mr Cluff is still wearing his Tam o' Shanter, trotting around the playground like a happy pony. He keeps talking about *Katherine this* and *Katherine that*, but never *Katherine is coming home*. Has **MISSION McKENZIE** done nothing more than turn Mr Cluff into a mush-brained doofus??

Thursday, 26 July

The Colonel gave us another mind-sharpening survival challenge today. He gathered us all into his room, threw his arms into the air and shouted, 'Earthquake!'

Cassie screamed and threw herself under a desk.

The Colonel leaned forward and said, 'You are hiking through the mountains in Mongolia. Your pack yak starts to bellow and stomp around. Suddenly the ground begins to shake. You are caught in the middle of a violent earthquake. The rock beneath you splits and you find your feet planted on either side of a widening chasm. The chasm is so deep that you cannot see the bottom. Your forehead breaks out in terrified beads of sweat. Your legs cannot stretch much further. Could this be the end? You feel in your pocket and all you have is an apple, a pair of tweezers and some superglue. What will you do?'

Mat rolled her eyes and said, 'Well, *obviously*, there's not much I *could* do. I can't use the tweezers to pluck my eyebrows if I don't have a mirror. Duh!'

Banjo shook his head in despair and said, 'Mongolia is *another* word that's really hard to rhyme with. Like orange and rhinoceros.'

Gabby said, 'Why aren't I carrying bandages? There should always be bandages in my pockets!'

Jack jumped up yelling, 'I know! I'd use the superglue to stick the crack back together again. Then I couldn't fall down it and I'd live happily ever after, eating my apple.'

The Colonel explained that, while it *was* superglue, it wasn't *superhero* glue.

Grace said, 'I really don't think I'd have taken a yak with me. I would have taken a pony. Maybe even two or three ponies. They're much prettier than yaks.'

So much for getting us to use our brains in an emergency!

The Colonel wriggled his hairy eyebrows and said, 'I'd use the apple to coax the yak to come to me. While he was munching, I would grab the yak's horn with my other hand that I had smothered in superglue, so that it would stick and keep me firmly attached to him. Then I'd use the tweezers in my free hand to pluck some hair from the yak's bottom, giving him a fright so that he'd bolt away from the chasm, dragging me to safety.'

Everyone burst out laughing just thinking of the Colonel being dragged up and down the mountains stuck to the horn of a galloping yak. Still, it was a pretty cool idea.

Wes and Fez wanted to see how fast an alpaca could run this afternoon. Fez said, 'Ready … set …' and Wes plucked some hair from Macka's bum with tweezers.

Macka didn't run at all. He squealed, bit Wes on the shoulder and spat in Fez's face. Wes rolled around on the grass moaning. Macka trotted around gurgling merrily.

Friday, 27 July

Haven't got much for the next *Bake Tribulation* yet. Everyone is too excited about camp to think of anything else. Mat, Ben and I are hoping that Gumbledong Ridge will give plenty of ideas for articles and poems. I'll write a special camp feature for the front page when we get back.

Ben has been working hard on the next episode of 'Heart's Triumph' but he got a bit carried away with the blood and guts thing. During English he showed me what he'd written. Edmund had suffered so much at the hands of wild animals, vampires, flesh-eating aliens and werewolves that he had lost three arms, seven legs and fourteen toes. When I pointed this out to Ben, he got upset. He said I am the fussiest editor he's ever worked for and he doesn't want to write the romance any more.

What am I going to do now? I can't write 'Heart's Triumph' myself! That would be *too* stressful!

Saturday, 28 July

Mum had Sophie's old boarding school uniforms out today. Don't know why. Sophie is far too tall for them. Hope it's nothing to do with that big fat wool cheque that came during the week.

Hopefully Mum is going to give the uniforms away because she realises that I will NEVER need them. It's stupid to send me away to boarding school when I'm obviously doing just fine with online learning.

Wes, Fez and Smart Rat spent all day designing new tails for Gunther. Poor Gunther has been very quiet since the Great Chicken Coop Explosion on the Queen's Birthday. At first we thought it was just because he was sore where his tail had blown off, but that's healed now.

Gunther still fusses over his bunnies like a mother hen, and plays with them in the long grass. But he's no longer feral. He seems to have lost all his anger, and hasn't even *looked* like savaging Wes and Fez for weeks. It's devastating to see.

Sunday, 29 July

Gunther bit Fez, head-butted Wes and ate Smart Rat today. I don't think he liked the hot-glue gun being used to stick his new tail on. Still, it's good to see the old Gunther back in action again.

Wes and Fez don't seem too worried about Smart Rat. I thought they'd be heartbroken, but Wes said Smart Rat was stupid to use hot glue on Gunther's bum.

'A smart rat is cool as,' said Wes.

'But a dumb rat is lame,' said Fez.

'We were starting to suspect that he couldn't even read,' said Wes.

'Or say his nine times tables,' said Fez.

We're all packed for camp. I've added a bag of jelly babies and Dad's pocketknife to my backpack.

Wes and Fez went to bed wearing jeans, jumpers, raincoats and tea cosies on their heads.

They won't let anyone look at what's in their backpacks. They're probably full of dead animals and sheep droppings. Mum said it will be their own fault if they've left something important behind.

Matilda Jane the Mature rang Sophie tonight. They spoke for nearly an hour trying to work out which nail polish colours were the most important ones for Mat to take on camp and which ones she might be able to live without for two days. I sure hope I am never stuck with Mat in a real crisis situation. Now *that* would be terrifying.

Monday, 30 July
8.30 am

We are on our way!

I'm sitting up the back of the bus with Banjo, Ben, Mat and Davo. Mat is putting Cherry Romance nail polish on Davo's fingernails. Mrs Gillies, Tom's mum, is driving the bus. The Colonel is sitting up the front telling wild adventure stories to the little kids. I just heard him say something about overcoming the Terrible Turkey Plague of Trinidad in 2003 by celebrating Christmas for twenty-seven days in a row!

Mr Cluff is sitting alone in his Tam o' Shanter, humming 'Scotland the Brave'. It sounds dreadful — nearly as bad as the bagpipes.

The carrier pigeons are all in their special travel cage, except for Feathers, who is stuffed up Worms's jumper to keep warm.

Tom has just let his frog loose from the little tin he carries in his pocket. It's hopping towards the front of the bus.

11 am

On our way again.

We've just had our morning tea break in the park at Coonabarabran. Worms ate two egg sandwiches, an apple and three chocolate bars. His backpack is stuffed full of food.

Harry spent the whole time at the park scooping these big orange and white fish out of the pond. He said European carp are a real pest and should never be allowed to live anywhere in Australia. He's absolutely right, but it turned out that these particular fish weren't European carp at all. They were rare and expensive Japanese goldfish.

The park manager wasn't too happy.

Gabby did her best to revive each fish by giving it mouth-to-mouth resuscitation. They

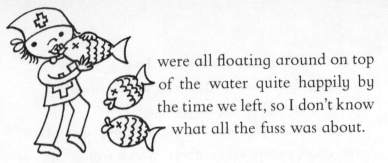

were all floating around on top of the water quite happily by the time we left, so I don't know what all the fuss was about.

11.40 am

The Colonel has got us making up silly songs, so I will write the words down as we go:

Gong-dongle-diggery-dam
I like a sandwich with cheese and ham
I butter it twice and cut it up small
And sail it down the waterfall

Gong-dongle-buffety-beam
I like a sandwich with cherries and cream
I dip it in milk and fold it in four
And smear it all over the kitchen floor

Gong-dongle-zippety-zoo
I like a sandwich with rabbit poo
I spread it with pickles both front and back
And drive it down the railway track

Gong-dongle-diggery-dunny
I like a sandwich with peas and honey
I water it with the garden hose
And use it to scrub the mud off my toes

Gong-dongle-fluffety-fam
I like a sandwich with eggs and jam
I wrap it in paper and bubble gum
Then use it at once to wipe my bum

Mr Cluff made us stop after Jack sang the last verse, because Worms laughed until he threw up his entire morning tea.

Gross.

1.30 pm — Gumbledong Ridge

Arrived here in time for a picnic lunch.

The Colonel gave us a very serious safety talk, then handed us each a compass, a chocolate frog and a bright fluorescent yellow vest so that we can be easily seen. He said, 'We don't want anyone to get lost in the bush.'

That's not *quite* true. I wouldn't mind if Wes and Fez were lost for a couple of days … or weeks …

The Colonel explained that this is private property, so there are no walking paths through the bush or up around the ridge. We need to stick together to keep safe. The compasses are *just-in-case*.

Mr Cluff sent Davo and Nick off towards the gully to dig a hole and set up the toilet. It's really cool — just like our old outdoor dunny, but it's a tent and the toilet seat is set up over a small hole that we'll fill in with dirt before we leave.

We had a competition to see who could pitch their tent first. Mat, Lucy, Dora and I came second. Ned, Worms, Gary and Ben were first, but a gust of wind swept through the camp soon after, and their tent blew into the creek. Serves them right for not using the tent pegs and ropes.

We're just waiting for them to hang their sleeping bags up to dry before we head off up the ridge.

8.40 pm

Had a fantastic afternoon doing rock climbing and abseiling along the ridge. We had to walk quite a way to find a stable cliff. There are lots of crumbly bits and rockslides in this area.

Cassie got scared halfway up the rock wall and had to be rescued by the Colonel, but everyone else loved it. All that scrambling over the roof at home has really paid off for Wes and Fez. They scuttled up and down the cliff like goannas.

On the way back to camp we came across a herd of wild goats. They got such a fright that they stampeded up the ridge, sending rocks tumbling down all over the place. One hit Dora on the foot and, before we knew what had happened, Gabby had bandaged Dora's foot, leg and head, and had Nick and Ned carrying her home on a stretcher made from two long sticks and *my* coat. Dora kept saying, 'It doesn't even hurt,' but Gabby said it was the shock talking.

When we got back to camp it was time to build a fire and cook our tea. Sausages cooked on sticks held over an open fire are the best. Just ask Worms. He ate nine of them!

Blacky, Greyey and Patch were set free with messages to carry home to Hardbake Plains to our parents. The Colonel let Sam, Nick and Lucy write the notes.

Lucy wrote *Had a great day. We are all safe and happy. I love you, Mummy and Daddy.*

Nick wrote *Nick loves Lynette.*

Sam wrote *Somebody please talk to my worms. They will be lonely.*

Lucy was worried that the pigeons wouldn't find their way in the dark, but the Colonel said they'll be fine. They have that magnetite in their brain that acts like a compass.

We're all tucked up in our sleeping bags now. I'm writing this by torchlight. Lucy, Mat and Dora are eating my jelly babies.

Goodnight, Camp Gumbledong.

11.25 pm

Lucy and Dora can't get to sleep. They're scared after the camp-fire stories of yowies. Mat is calming them down by telling them *Hansel and Gretel*.

Good choice. A story about two little children who get LOST in the DEEP DARK FOREST, then captured by a WICKED WITCH who wants to EAT them won't be at all scary.

Goodnight again, Camp Gumbledong.

Tuesday, 31 July
2.35 am!!!

Just got Lucy and Dora to sleep at 2 am when we were all woken by an ear-piercing scream.

It turns out that Davo and Nick thought they'd save time and energy digging the hole for the toilet by setting it up over a wombat burrow! Sarah crept off to use the loo in the middle of the night and was interrupted by a wombat waddling out of his home. Knocked her clean off.

Sarah ran out screaming, 'I'm never ever going to the loo again!'

The wombat sprinted through the camp, grunting and snuffling in terror. He ran right over the top of Ned, Worms, Gary and Ben who were sleeping under the stars.

Sarah is now in *our* tent, snuggled in between Mat and Dora.

Goodnight *again*, Camp Gumbledong.

3.20 am

Wes woke me at 3 am, bawling his eyes out.

'It's Smart Rat,' he sobbed. 'He was thick as a brick but I still loved him.'

He howled, 'I really miss him!'

I patted him on the back for a while but he just wouldn't stop crying.

Fez woke up, missed Wes and came over to our tent. He tried to cuddle up to Wes, but Wes pushed him away and called him a sissy pink-pants. Fez got upset and punched Wes, and they started rumbling. They wrestled over the top of Mat and she didn't even wake up! She just kept snoring like a steam engine.

I finally calmed them down and stopped Wes crying. I think they are just about asleep now.

Our tent is bulging at the seams.

Goodnight *again*, Camp Gumbledong!!!

8.20 am

Our tent collapsed on top of us at 7 am. I think seven people in a four-man tent was just too much. Especially when Lucy started sleepwalking.

I'm a bit tired this morning, but the bush is beautiful at the start of the day. There were three fat wallabies on the edge of our camp and two eastern rosellas perched on the Colonel and Mr Cluff's tent.

The wombat was totally confused and had torn the toilet tent that was blocking his burrow. Ben and I had to take the tent down, then give him some space so that he felt safe enough to go back home for the day.

Had a fascinating lesson on open-air toilets before breakfast. The Colonel handed out small shovels and said it is good to bury whatever you deposit in the bush. He wriggled his eyebrows like two hairy caterpillars and nodded meaningfully.

About two minutes later Mat finally understood what the new toilet arrangement was and said, 'Ooooh gross!' Everyone else burst out laughing.

I'm writing this as I feed a kookaburra my bacon rind from breakfast. He's really cute. Every time I toss him a piece, he grabs it in his beak and whacks it on a rock as though he needs to kill it before eating it. Just like he did with Tom's frog.

10.35 am

We are waiting to head off on our big hike for the day. We would have left an hour ago except Ned and Sam got into a sticky situation.

Ned wanted to be prepared for anything at camp, including an earthquake. He had packed an apple, some tweezers and a tube of superglue. Don't know where he planned to pick up a yak ...

Unfortunately, the tube of superglue burst when he pulled it out of his pack this morning. It went everywhere. His pack ended up stuck to his chest and his hands got stuck to his sleeping bag when he tried to wipe them clean. Sam came to help and his hands got stuck to Ned's. They fell over and ended up with the apple and tweezers stuck to Sam's bum.

The Colonel and Mr Cluff were puzzling over what to do, when Matilda Jane the Mature sat down on a rock nearby and started removing her Bluebell Bliss nail polish. The Colonel shouted with joy. Apparently nail polish remover is perfect for dissolving superglue.

Mat said she couldn't *possibly* give them her nail polish remover. It was the only bottle she had with her. Mr Cluff explained that Ned and Sam couldn't possibly go hiking up Gumbledong Ridge glued to a sleeping bag, a backpack, an apple, a pair of tweezers and each other, and maybe — just maybe — she could live without perfect fingernails for one day.

Mat was horrified at the thought. While she was rolling her eyes and fanning her face, Mr Cluff snatched the nail polish remover from her hands.

The Colonel and Mr Cluff are dealing with Sam and Ned now.

Gabby is treating Mat for shock.

1.20 pm

Sitting on a rock in the middle of the thick bush, halfway around Gumbledong Ridge.

What a great morning. We just got into our walk when Cassie screamed, 'Yowie!'

She was right. Below us in the trees we could see *three* yowies! The Colonel had been out first thing this morning and set up three giant yowie shapes made out of cardboard. He brought out the archery gear and we spent an hour shooting the yowies before they could scramble up the rocks to eat us for their breakfast.

How cool was that?! It was like being in the middle of an action movie.

We've just had Vegemite sandwiches and bananas for lunch and now we're nibbling on scroggin. Scroggin is this really yummy mix that the Colonel made up with dried fruit, nuts and bits of chocolate. It's meant to give you lots of energy for hiking.

3.10 pm

Disaster!

We're on our own.

Separated from the others.

Stranded.

It's all Mat's fault.

We were scrambling along a steep part of the ridge and everything was going just fine until Matilda Jane the Mature screamed. It sounded like her arm was being torn off by a wild haggis, but she'd just chipped her fingernail on the edge of a rock.

Her scream was so loud that it scared a herd of wild goats hiding in the bush. They bolted in fright, through the middle of us all, straight up the ridge, loosening bits of the cliff with their feet as they went.

At first, just a few rocks were tumbling down, but then more started to fall, then bigger rocks, until finally we could hear something rumbling like thunder above us.

Mr Cluff yelled, 'Avalanche! Run!'

So we did.

I don't know how we got out of the way in time. All I can say is that scroggin must have some superpowered ingredients in it. I grabbed

Worms and just about carried him back the way we had come, leaping over rocks. I dragged Gabby behind me by the straps of her backpack. All I could hear was ear-splitting sounds as rocks smashed against each other and tumbled down the ridge. It went on and on, getting noisier and noisier, chasing us back along the ridge.

When I couldn't run another step, I dragged Gabby and Worms against a boulder and hugged them to me. I closed my eyes and waited for the thundering noise to stop.

When I opened my eyes again, all I could see were millions of rocks, trees snapped like toothpicks, and Gabby, Worms, Wes, Fez and Mat.

Of *all* the people I could have been stranded with today it had to include Wes, Fez and Matilda Jane the Mature.

What a disaster!

3.50 pm

We've yelled and screamed for half an hour but no-one has answered. They could be miles away on the other side of the rockslide.

At least I *hope* they're all on the other side.

Anything else is just too horrible to think about.

Wes and Fez reckon the Colonel knows how to survive anything. I hope they're right.

But what about us?

We can't go across the rockslide. It's far too unstable.

The Colonel told us that the best thing to do if you get lost is to wait where you are. Help will come.

So that's what we're doing.

Waiting.

4.15 pm

Still waiting.

Wes found a baby goat by the edge of the rockslide. Its leg is cut and it can't walk properly. It must have been separated from the herd and got swept down on the edge of the avalanche. Poor little thing.

Gabby is giving it first aid. It'll probably end up with its tail in a sling, its head bandaged and its tonsils removed!

Mat is sitting on a boulder, filing her fingernails.

Waiting.

4.50 pm

Still waiting.

It will be getting dark soon.

Mat said what if the others didn't make it past the rockslide? What if no-one is coming to help us? We can't wait forever.

She's right.

We *can't* wait forever.

8.10 pm

We're lost.

Totally lost.

In the middle of the bush.

In the dark.

Alone.

Exhausted.

We decided we had to find our own way back to camp. I knew it was south. I'm sure we followed the compass south, but we should be back by now if we walked in the right direction.

Worms has eaten three muesli bars, an apple and two chocolate frogs from his backpack. Kitty the kid has eaten Worms's apple core. I shared my block of chocolate with the others but it wasn't enough.

We're lost and hungry.

9.30 pm

We've stopped to set up camp for the night. That's what the Colonel would do.

Wes, Fez, Gabby and I gathered twigs, sticks and logs for a fire but the dew had already made everything wet. I used nearly all my matches trying to light it but it was just too damp.

Gabby is worried that Kitty the kid will get hypothermia. She's wrapped her from head to toe in bandages to keep out the cold.

I'm worried that the rest of us will get hypothermia.

9.50 pm

We're all wearing tea cosies. Except for Mat. She said it is too humiliating to be running around the bush looking like a teapot.

Wes's backpack was full of tea cosies and ropes. Mat said he should have packed something useful, like a blanket or a mobile phone. But I really don't think she can talk. Her pack is full of nail polish, lip gloss, shampoo, conditioner, brushes, tweezers, eyelash curlers, four *Girl Alive* magazines, a novel called *Kisses Under the Rainbow* and a blow drier. Where on earth did she think she was going to plug in a blow drier? That girl can be such a twit!

Anyway, at least our heads are warm, even if the rest of our bodies are freezing.

10.30 pm

We have fire!

Worms ate the rest of the food in his pack — a bag of peanuts, another three muesli bars, two bags of chips and two bananas. He rifled through Gabby's backpack looking for more supplies, but it's just full of bandages and other first aid stuff.

Worms started to go into shock at the thought of spending all night without any food, so Gabby pulled a little jar of butter from her pocket and gave it to him. He was just about to scoff it down when I grabbed it.

Butter is fat and fat burns.

I tore the pages from *Kisses Under the Rainbow*, smeared them with butter and stuffed them at the bottom of our fire. I used my last two matches and the buttery paper caught alight. The twigs crackled, the flames licked the sticks and a lovely, warming fire sprang to life. What a relief!

Mat is cheesed off about her book.

Worms is cheesed off about the butter.

At least we have fire for light and warmth.

Maybe in the morning we can use it to make smoke signals.

10.55 pm

The baby goat has just eaten one of Mat's *Girl Alive* magazines.

Mat is really cheesed off.

So is Worms. He had no idea you could eat *Girl Alive*, and is quite angry that Mat won't let him eat the other three magazines.

11.15 pm

Worms has just pulled Feathers out of his jumper!

He keeps looking from Feathers to the camp fire and back again, licking his lips. I think he's dreaming of roast pigeon.

11.30 pm

I'm dreaming of roast pigeon. We're all starving and getting colder by the minute, despite our big fire.

192

Mat is writing an SOS note to put in Feathers' little message capsule. If he flies home, our mums and dads will know that we're still alive and need rescuing.

11.45 pm
Feathers won't fly home. Every time we toss him up into the air he flaps about and lands back on Worms's shoulder. He just wants to get back down his jumper where it's nice and warm.

Can't say I blame him. It's FREEZING, even with the fire blazing.

Mat has finally given up and put the purple owl tea cosy with the goggly eyes on her head.

Midnight
We keep hearing dreadful growling noises. I think it's Worms's tummy rumbling but Gabby, Wes and Fez are convinced there are yowies lurking in the bush. They're digging a pit trap with the little toilet shovels so that if a yowie stomps through the bush towards the fire to eat us, it will fall down the pit and we'll be safe.

Yeah, right. The whole pit trap thing worked so well on the foxes at Hillrose Poo, didn't it????

12.25 am

Feathers is on his way!

Mat was plucking her eyebrows — because that's what you do when you're dying of starvation and hypothermia — when Wes got the brilliant idea. He and Fez climbed as high as they could up a gumtree. They dragged Feathers up to them in a pulley made from ropes and a tea cosy. Fez held Feathers out in his hands while Wes used the tweezers to pluck his tail. Feathers squawked in shock, flapped up into the air and disappeared.

He hasn't returned so we're hoping that he's on his way to Hardbake Plains.

Maybe we won't die out here after all.

1.15 am

Worms was so hungry, he ate Mat's cherry-flavoured lip gloss. Then he started on her apple-scented shampoo. He was frothing at the mouth!

Mat was furious. She tied him up with Wes's rope so that he can't interfere with any more of her precious beauty products. She used three overhand knots, two figure-eight knots, then finished off with an exploding knot just to make sure he can't get free. The Colonel's outdoor adventure lessons really have come in handy.

1.30 am

Worms is on the loose again. He and Kitty the kid are nibbling on the May issue of *Girl Alive*.

Wes set him free. He was worried that if the exploding knot actually exploded it would blow Worms's hands off.

1.45 am

There are *definitely* growling, grunting noises coming from the bush. Worms's tummy is growling heaps but there are noises coming from the other side of the fire too.

Yowies aren't real ... are they????

3 am

Emptied our pockets just to make sure no-one had any food that they had forgotten about. Fez had a Lego car, a mouse tail, seven marbles and a little tin full of rabbit poo. Wes had a pair of clean undies in each of his pockets. Worms's pockets were stuffed full of empty chip packets and muesli bar wrappers.

I had three spare pens for writing in my diary and a dirty hanky. What would the Colonel have to say about the dirty hanky?

Mat had a mirror and Pearly Pink waterproof lipstick. It's great to know that if we get chased by a rhinoceros and end up on the edge of a crocodile-infested river, Mat will have everything we need to survive …

I wanted to check Fez's backpack but he won't take it off and refuses to let anyone near it. He said it is private and nobody's business.

3.40 am

Growling noises coming from all around. Worms's tummy or the yowies?

I'm frozen. I can hardly move my fingers to write this, but if we die I want people to know what our final hours were like. If Burke and Wills could leave a diary behind, so can I …

4.05 am

Gabby has bandaged everyone's arms and legs for warmth.

Wes and Fez are discussing how to use Kitty the kid as a hat.

Kitty is eating Worms's muesli bar wrappers.

We have been singing camp-fire songs to keep our minds off how cold and hungry we are:

Gong-dongle-diggery-dote
I like a sandwich with baby goat
I toast it twice and cut it up thinner
And gobble it up for a nice hot dinner

It hasn't worked.
I'm scared.
What if we don't survive?

August

Wednesday, 1 August
10.30 am — Hillrose Poo, in bed,
rescued and alive!

And it's all thanks to Wes and Fez!

Early this morning, after Wes and Fez decided that Kitty was too small and too injured to use as a hat, Fez said they should cuddle up to use each other's body warmth. Wes pushed him away and told him not to be a sissy pinkpants.

Fez said they would die of hypothermia if they didn't snuggle together, and hugged Wes with all his might. He threw in a kiss for good luck. Wes shoved and struggled but Fez clung on. They rolled around on the ground, punching and pushing, until Wes tore Fez's tea cosy and backpack off and threw them into the fire.

The backpack sizzled and quickly caught alight. A big hole burnt out of the side and, suddenly, our camp fire burst into action!

198

Pink, orange, green and yellow fireworks began to spray out like a supersonic fountain. Shooting balls flew up in the air and exploded into showers of stars. Other balls shot into the sky, screaming and howling until they exploded with a bang and scattered sparks all over the bush. Fez screamed with fury and disappointment as his secret end-of-camp fireworks display went off in one enormous exhibition.

A wild pig and her piglet, terrified by the noise and flashes of light, ran through the bush squealing, and fell straight down the yowie trap. The mother pig scrambled out and charged after us.

We were still running around in our tea cosies and bandages, trying to escape the angry pig, when Dad, the Colonel, Mr Cluff and three police rescue workers stepped into the light of our fire. The fireworks had given the best SOS signal ever and led them straight to our camp.

Gabby fainted with relief.

Worms said, 'Has anyone got any food?'

Mat stepped towards the angry pig, shoved her lipstick up its snout, leapfrogged over its back and ran until she fell face first down the yowie trap on top of the piglet.

Wes, Fez and I threw ourselves into Dad's arms.

Saved at last!

7.15 pm

Matilda Jane the Mature has just rung in tears. Our rescue was on the national news and Mat was filmed walking out of the bush with a purple, goggle-eyed owl tea cosy on her head, pig snot on her face and bandages all over her arms and legs. Her fly was undone.

'I'm going to die!' she cried.

'The whole country has seen me with my fly down and a tea cosy on my head,' she moaned.

'And pig snot on your face,' I reminded her.

She hung up!

Friday, 3 August

Such a busy time getting today's edition of *The Bake Tribulation* ready. There has been so much to organise. Contributions poured in and I think we may have our best paper ever.

In addition to my own special camp run-down, we have three more exciting reports. 'Magnetite at Gumbledong' explains the discovery by the search and rescue teams that compasses *just don't work* along the ridge. Great information but given THREE DAYS TOO LATE!

'Feathered friend' tells of how Feathers arrived home *today* at lunch time. He looked like he'd flown through a hailstorm, dog-paddled through mud and been run over by a lawn mower. He delivered Mat's note that said, 'Help. We are five children and one attractive young lady lost in the bush near Gumbledong Ridge.' Gabby was quite upset that *another* group was in the same horrible situation as we'd been in. She grabbed her first aid kit, three blankets and a thermometer, and was setting off to help before Mr Cluff managed to explain the situation.

'Hardbake Plains' very own superstar' tells about Mat's unusual rescue photo being on *twenty-seven* different internet news sites. People all over Australia are asking where they can purchase one of those hilarious tea cosies in the shape of an owl. You'd think Mat would be pleased with the fame, but she keeps bursting into tears and saying, 'I wish I'd never been rescued.' Now *there's* a thought …

We have several articles giving helpful advice, including 'What fish is that?' by Harry, 'Travelling with frogs' by Tom, 'Bush toilets — the ugly truth' by Sarah, and 'Pitching tents — the essentials' by Gary. It's great to see that we can all learn from our mistakes.

Banjo has contributed *three* fabulous poems.

Night-time Terror

Have you ever done a poo
In a wombat burrow loo?
Sarah has and thought it a disaster.
The wombat got a fright
And bolted through the night
But Sarah bolted through the night
   much faster.

Fussy Fish

Fish are fussy creatures,
They like a lot of water,
And if you take them out
They don't wriggle like they ought to.

They flap a bit and flounder,
And slowly fall asleep,
And float around quite lazily
When chucked back in the creek.

It doesn't matter if they're carp
Or Japanese exotics,
When it comes to keeping fish alert,
There's gotta be aquatics.

You can try to give them mouth to mouth
Or say a little prayer,
But fishies just need water
'Cause they drown from pure air.

Superglue

Superglue can spring a leak,
When from the tube it races,
Sticking everything you touch
To inconvenient places.
A sleeping bag sticks to your hands
Your tweezers to your thumb,
Your friend can stick onto your chest,
An apple to your bum.
It makes it very difficult
To sit down on a chair
Or lie in bed or wash your face
Or even comb your hair.
So listen up my friends –
No matter what you do,
Before you head out camping
Throw away the superglue.

Grace has written a story about three ponies, a kitten and a wombat, and Tom's latest survey is sure to be popular:

Which animal would you least like to pop up in your toilet?

❏ a wombat
❏ a frog
❏ a grasshopper
❏ a yowie
❏ a carrier pigeon
❏ a rabbit
❏ a haggis

The classifieds are full of interesting local information, as usual:

WORMS vs KITTY THE KID

Exciting eating challenge.
Has Worms met his match?
Find out who is the biggest garbage guts.
School playground
Lunch time
Tuesday 4 August

Matilda Jane the Mature couldn't bear the thought of her romance serial not being finished, so she kindly stepped in at the last minute to write the final episode. She was determined to create something that will have everyone talking. And I think everyone *will* be talking about it for

205

quite some time. Ben's had a spot of trouble with the printing again. Some of the text from our other articles doubled up over the top of 'Heart's Triumph'. It's funny how that happens …

Heart's Triumph — Part 5

Edmund lay on the ground in agony, but he did not want to distress his beloved Elizabeth. He sat up, cringing with the pain, but managed to put a smile on his overwhelmingly handsome face.

'My darling,' he sighed, heavy of heart. 'Life with just one arm and one leg is going to be tough.

It makes it very difficult
To sit down on a chair
Or lie in bed or wash your face
Or even comb your hair.

There will be many months of painful medical treatment. But together, we can seek top quality vet care at a reasonable price, *if only you can stand the sight of me.'*

Edmund began to sob in a totally manly, handsome, romantic sort of way.

Elizabeth cried, 'Oh Edmund, my darling. We will travel this journey together. I'm sure there is so much we can learn from each other, like how to break wind without people thinking you are rude.

Just look shocked and blame the noise on the dog, the squeaky chair or your brother.'

Edmund smiled with relief.

'Dearest, darling Elizabeth,' he sighed. 'You are too, too kind. I just have one more thing I need to ask of you ...'

He knelt on his one remaining knee, took her hand in his one remaining hand, looked deeply into her eyes and asked, 'Does your pig have diarrhoea?'

Elizabeth cried, 'Yes! Oh yes!'

Edmund replied, 'You have made me the happiest man alive.'

THE END

A fascinating conclusion that is sure to give our readers much joy. But not nearly as much joy as the VERY BEST NEWS EVER to reach the pages of *The Bake Tribulation*:

PUBLIC ANNOUNCEMENT

Katherine McKenzie will be returning to Hardbake Plains on Friday 17 August.

MISSION McKENZIE accomplished.

I have a really good feeling about the rest of this year!

Saturday, 4 August

AAAAAAAAAAAAAAAHHHHH!!

Mega bummer.

The traitors are sending me to boarding school.

HELP!!!!!

About the author

Katrina Nannestad grew up in central west New South Wales. After studying arts and education at the University of New England in Armidale, she worked as a primary school teacher. Her first teaching job was at a tiny two-teacher school in the bush. Katrina now lives near Bendigo with her husband, two sons and a pea-brained whippet.

Have you read all of Blue's adventures?

Blue Weston's life is spiralling out of control.

* Her parents are sending her to boarding school next year.
* Her mad twin brothers are building pig chariots in the back shed.
* Her best friend has been abducted by zombies and replaced with a boy-crazy tween.
* And then there's the drought that's showing no signs of ending soon ...

It's New Year's Day, and Blue has resolved to keep a diary of the year's events. It will be another hard year of dust storms and drought on her family's farm — with the odd leech attack and bagpipe-loving pig thrown in for good measure!

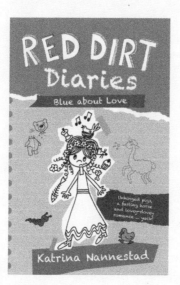

I'm going to be a bridesmaid.
Mat, Lynette and me.
Long, pink shiny dresses and flowers in our hair.
Leading Miss McKenzie down the aisle to disaster.
I think I'm going to puke ...

When Blue's favourite teacher announces she's engaged, Blue thinks she must have lost her mind. Why would Miss McKenzie want to get married? Especially to someone named James Linley Welsh-Pearson! Surely it couldn't be because she loves him — could it?

Can Blue stop the wedding in time or will Miss McKenzie leave Hardbake Plains ... forever?